NOBLE LEGEND

JACK NOBLE BOOK FOURTEEN

L.T. RYAN

LIQUID MIND MEDIA

THE JACK NOBLE SERIES

For paperback purchase links, visit:
https://ltryan.com/pb

CHAPTER 1

THE MAN IN THE WORN LEATHER JACKET EXITED THE building five minutes before the explosion rocked a street corner on the outskirts of Barcelona. Far from the Gothic district. Far from Gaudí. Tourists didn't visit this section of town. No one did. The only people who would perish were those no one cared about. No one important.

He ducked into a cafe, ordered an Americano. Used an American accent. The young woman behind the counter rolled her eyes and asked for his name. He told her *John*, not that it was the truth. Then he stepped into the bathroom and slipped off his backpack. It hit the counter with a solid *thunk*. The thick false bottom that hid his Glock.

The zipper stuck, so he jiggled it, working the stray thread free from the tracks. Inside were a few folders and two lockboxes. The biometric lock recognized his thumb print and disengaged. The lid popped open. Gold light didn't spill out of the lockbox like in the movies, but the four steel cards, each with twenty-four random words etched into them, were worth more than any amount of gold he could fit into such a small space. They were the passphrases to four of ten crypto wallets. In the second lockbox, a digital screen displayed an aggregate balance of a quarter of a billion dollars in Bitcoin spread across the ten wallets.

His accomplice had been correct. And was now dead.

He had a moment of doubt. Not concern over those who might be in the building. They meant nothing. Had he been seen, though? Had he put enough distance between himself and the building?

He thought of Lorraine's parting words when he left Amsterdam a month prior to track the men who had stolen the money from the Vatican. *"This is our chance at freedom. A chance to start a new life, Dylan. We can have a family. Don't get caught."*

If he was close enough to the action, no one would suspect him. And why would they? He was nobody in the city of five-and-a-half million. Over forty-one thousand per square mile. Anyone could get lost in the shuffle here.

The second lockbox also contained a cell phone. He wouldn't use it to make a call, though. He pinched the bridge of his nose, clenched his eyelids tight, pressed the button on the bottom half of the screen. The button that would complete his cover up.

The explosion and subsequent aftershock rocked the café as he stepped back into the dining room. His to-go cup skittered off the counter and hit the floor. The lid shot off, and his Americano spread across the maroon tiles.

Everyone looked up from their laptops, phones, and even a few newspapers and magazines. The young woman with the attitude and dark eyes now focused those eyes, wide with fear, on him.

He returned the look. "The hell was that?" Fortunately, he had practiced the phrase prior to leaving the restroom so his accent wouldn't slip out.

"Sounds like a bus slammed into our building!" She looked out at the street, at the dozens of people turned to the east, hands shielding their eyes from the sun as they searched for the source of the sound.

He reached down and picked up the now empty to-go cup and placed it on the counter before leaving the café.

Outside, the scene had turned frantic. Sirens wailed, echoing off the five- and six-story buildings that lined the street. Fire trucks, ambulances, police cars raced past. People jumped out of their way at the last minute in some cases.

Everyone spoke quickly, making it difficult to decipher their Catalan dialect, a dialect he had trouble picking up in any conversation. What he could make out indicated no one had a clue what had happened. Plane crash. Chemical explosion. Bombing downtown. All speculation. They were close enough to feel the impact, but far enough that all they had in view was a dark cloud of smoke choking the sky.

They'd know soon. The footage would emerge. His face might appear on the news. Soon. It wouldn't matter once the body was found.

He had to create distance from the decimated building. Using the edge of his hand like a blade, he sliced through the gathering crowd while another group of fire trucks, ambulances, and police cruisers raced past. The crowd offered anonymity. He used that to his advantage, remaining in the middle as he worked his way west.

His phone had been buzzing against his thigh since he left the café. After walking four blocks west and two north, he ducked into an alley and checked his text messages.

Job complete.

Cameras turned off.

Emergency comms down.

Get back to Amsterdam, any way possible.

Arrangements had been made in advance. Tickets for five different flights from three different airports. Train reservations from multiple stations. And three rental cars. All under different aliases. He feared all had been compromised.

That's why he had a backup plan.

He reached into his pocket and pulled out a set of keys. Cars of every color and make lined the street. He held his thumb on the panic button until a horn blared in the distance. A short walk later, he found the late-model BMW sandwiched between two other vehicles.

He continued on another block, stopped, waited, watched. Then he went another block to be safe. There were no tails. No one was following. Not physically. Cameras monitored every inch of the city. *Cameras shut off,* the text had read. He had to trust that was the case.

Taking his first deep breath of the morning, he turned back toward the vehicle. The two-block walk felt like it was two miles. Everything had gone to plan. That didn't matter. It only took one bystander with a phone to ruin plans.

The next step? Get out of Barcelona. Immediately.

CHAPTER 2

"A couple of weeks, Jack. At most. That's what we need. Can you lay low with us until then?"

Those were the last words Clarissa said to me after ushering Mia onto a private jet to reunite her with my brother, Sean. I questioned why it was necessary. The answer was simple. They had to go dark. And if I was to help, I had to as well.

Clarissa and Beck had found us in the Florida Keys. We were all together for a few days during which time they outlined the job ahead. Over two-hundred million dollars had been stolen from the Vatican in funds and several items, some priceless, had been taken as well. A few had shown up on the black market and had been returned. But the money had vanished. They theorized it had gone into an unmarked account and then moved into cryptocurrency. They thought it might be an inside job. They needed me to do things they were legally unable to do.

I spent the rest of the time hugging Mia, knowing she would be taken away from me soon.

Standing on the tarmac of a private runway, I felt the heat rising from the blacktop. Mia stopped at the stairs leading to the aircraft. She looked back at me, tears slipping down her cheeks. I ran to her. A few hushed words. A hug and a kiss. An I love you. Then that was it. She went up the stairs, flanked by two of Beck's men, and the small plane took off. An hour later, Clarissa, Beck, and I were somewhere over the Atlantic, en route to a safehouse in Belgium.

It was in Belgium, standing next to the Gulfstream as it refueled, while a driver waited for us at a distance, that Clarissa and Beck dropped the truth bomb. Their lead had been erased a few months prior, seemingly from existence. Beck said the instructions from the top of the chain of command were to abandon the operation. The same op that crossed paths with Clive Swift and his team while they were busy hunting me and Bear down. I had become mixed up in Beck and Clarissa's plans, whether purposefully or coincidentally. It all ended with Clarissa diving off the same pier in Genoa where I lay knocked out cold.

"So, what's the plan?" I asked.

Clarissa averted her gaze. She had no response.

"At least tell me when you received the directive to stand down."

She still wouldn't look at me. "Beck received it before we put Mia on that plane."

"Dammit, Clarissa." I laced my fingers behind my head and turned away.

She grabbed my shoulder. "I know, Jack. And I'm sorry, but you have to look at this from our point of view. We have a ton of evidence."

"Clearly."

She shook her head. "Let me finish."

"As far as I'm concerned, you already have."

Her hand slid to my forearm and she pulled me toward her. "Jack, this is just a temporary setback. We have experts on blockchain working to find the transactions and trace what we believe are the wallets where the Bitcoin was deposited. And I promise you, the answers you are after, who was behind that manhunt, who is ultimately responsible for Sasha's death, it'll all come out in this."

"How can you know that?"

She had no answer.

"Because, if you can state that with such confidence, then maybe you already know. Is that the case?"

She released her grip on my arm. "Jack…"

"What?"

Her eyes wavered as she looked into mine. For a moment, we were back a decade ago, standing in her apartment in Manhattan. What I'd give for those simpler times. Do a job. Get paid. Move on to the next. Suited me much better than trying to be a hero, saving the world. When I didn't care, no one cared about me.

Life was perfect.

"I don't know that," she admitted while taking a step backward. "Look, you're free to go. We'll get you on a flight out of Brussels this evening, if you want."

I pointed at the Gulfstream. "What's wrong with that? Why don't you have it take me to wherever Mia is?"

She stared at the ground between us.

"Can't do that, right?" I said. "Tell me this. What happens if I get in that car with you, then later tonight, I disappear? Won't take me long to figure out where my brother is. And once I do, I'll take Mia, and no one will ever find us again."

"She's not with your brother." She looked up at me with wet eyes.

"What do you mean?"

"Not yet, Jack. The plan is for her to be returned to him once we've moved them out of Belize."

"You've gotta be kidding me." I tipped my head back and forced a laugh. It was clear now. I had no choice. "Of all people, Clarissa. Of all people, you're extorting me?"

"Don't look at it like that." Her face reddened. With embarrassment over her betrayal? Or some other reason? "We had to keep things close to the vest for obvious reasons. And you're only gonna be in waiting mode for a week or two, tops."

"You knew all along. You knew before you got to the Keys this was at best put on hold, and at worst, the op was canceled."

"It's because you'll be invaluable to us. You can do things we can't. We're going to put you somewhere where you will be in position to go the moment we say go. It just might take a little bit. Use that time to decompress. But we knew if you went back to a life with Mia, we'd lose you forever."

"Forever, huh?"

"Jack, I could see it in your eyes, on your face."

"What?"

"Happiness."

I almost stumbled backward. Was she right? Was that a wormhole I was prepared to crawl into, knowing I might resurface the angriest I'd ever been?

She continued. "You seemed at peace. And it tore me apart to pull you out of that. But we knew what kind of asset you are and can be in this op."

I crossed my arms, widened my stance, exhaled heavily. "I can't believe you did this."

She held my gaze. "For what it's worth, I'm sorry."

"That's not worth much anymore, Clarissa."

My options were limited. I could get on a plane and be back in D.C. no later than tomorrow. Call in a few favors and have Mia back with me inside a week. But then what? Up until this moment, I felt I could trust Clarissa. The others, I wasn't sure of, including Beck. And I definitely didn't trust his superiors. What damage would a refusal cause?

I wanted to scream. Years ago, I'd have said to hell with them all. There was no one else to worry about, except maybe Bear, and he could take care of himself. But now Mia had to be considered. And I was considering what might happen to her if I told Clarissa and Beck to go to hell.

Sensing my train of thought, Clarissa said, "You don't have many options. And I don't have a lot of answers for you one way or the other should you choose to leave. It's out of my hands now. It has been for longer than I care to admit."

"Who knows?"

"Knows what?"

"That I'm involved."

"Enough people know that it would be uncomfortable for you to abandon the op."

"That high up?"

"Not exactly, but you know how these things go. It's *need to know*, and while the higher-ups don't know about you now, if you were to leave with the knowledge you have, it would be upsetting for them when they found out."

"What's it matter? You said it was canceled anyway."

"That's only temporary. We'll be back in business soon."

I took a few steps back and stared up at the cloudy sky. A breeze whipped around us, mixing the cool air with the warmth coming off the jet engines.

"Not to rush you," Clarissa said. "But we need to know how to proceed."

I turned to face her and nodded. "Where are we headed?"

"Well, *you're* going to Bruges. We've rented a place for you to stay while you wait for the next steps."

"Next steps?"

As if on cue, Beck walked up, carrying a black duffel bag. He set it down between us. "Cash, clothes, phone, laptop, weapons."

"What every growing boy needs," I quipped.

Beck's lips thinned as he nodded. "I know this isn't what you expected, Jack."

"Not true," I said. "Wasn't sure what to expect."

"Certainly not this," he said. "And I apologize for that. But stick with us, at least for a few weeks, while we get reauthorization. The evidence is solid."

"Doesn't appear I have much choice."

Beck glanced at Clarissa, then back at me. "You always have a choice. If you decide to go home, nothing bad will come to you. We won't be able to reunite you with Mia straight away, though. For her protection, mostly, with you being back in the spotlight."

"I like to think of myself standing just outside of it."

"Be that as it may, you're on the radar of some powerful people." Beck put his hands on his hips and glanced up at the silvery sun trying to peek out from behind the clouds. "And that's why, if you stick with us, we'll help you."

"In what way?"

"You have my word, Jack, if you do your part—"

"My part? What the hell does that mean? Not like this is my fault or I owe anyone anything here. I've done my time. I've done a dozen peoples' time. I was out and for good."

Beck held up his hands in surrender. "Poor phrasing. Sorry. Look, if you help us with this, I pledge my full support in helping you avenge Sasha's death and bring down whoever was after you. I'll do it off the books if I have to."

"What about your boss? And his boss? They pledging support, too? Off the books, or otherwise?"

Beck stood motionless, said nothing. Clarissa couldn't even look at me.

"That's what I thought." I scooped the duffel off the ground and started toward the car. "See y'all in a few weeks in Bruges. Maybe."

CHAPTER 3

Clarissa stared out the window in the Gulfstream, taking in the Mediterranean and a trace of land in the distance. She wished she could cast her guilt into the clouds below the jet. She'd lied to Jack. There was a reason, of course. She considered it a good one. But she still felt that this could be the act that would sever their ties forever.

Beck slid into the seat across from her and set a drink down. He folded his arms on the table between them. She felt it tip slightly toward him. He followed her gaze out the window, then cleared his throat.

"You did what you had to do, Clarissa," he said.

She nodded and looked over at him. "I know. Doesn't mean I have to feel good about it."

"You'll feel good when we've reclaimed that money." He took a sip of his drink, bourbon by the looks of it, and grimaced against the bite of the liquor. "Jack is more than capable of handling this."

"We should have told him what he's really getting into in Bruges." She reached into the cubby beside her seat and pulled out her phone. After unlocking it, she swiped across the screens and her thumb hovered over the messaging app. "I should tell him now, Beck."

He reached across the table, placed his hand over the phone. "He'll bail on us if you do. We'll never get all the pieces in play if that happens. I've held a reservation on that house for a month now. If there's a ground zero outside of that building in Barcelona bombing, it's in Bruges. You can't tell me being in the house next door to that dumbass that talked too much is a bad thing."

"So what's your plan?" She placed her phone face down on the table. Beck glanced at it several times, while seemingly debating how he'd answer. Clarissa picked the phone up and showed him the screen. "Is this making you nervous? Do you think I'm recording this or something?"

He shrugged. "Thought might've crossed my mind that you placed a call or started your voice recorder." He took her in, eased back in his seat. "Not like it would be the first time."

"If you don't trust me, why are we still working together?"

He threw up his hands in defeat. "You're right. You win." Beck paused a beat or two, looked out the window, and took a few deep breaths. "I called my informant. You know, the big guy working for the Concerted Dynamics cover up?"

"The one that runs between Brussels and Bruges?"

"Yeah. So, he's the one that tipped me off that the local guy in Bruges was going to Barcelona to take part in a 'big job.' This all happened when that account we pegged as holding some of the funds stolen from the Vatican was drained."

Clarissa felt her cheeks burn at the revelation. "Why are you only telling me this now?"

"I shouldn't have kept it from you. But it was the right thing to do."

"How can you say that?"

"Because you might've dumped all this on Noble before we even got him here. Then what? He probably would have heard about the bombing and the drained account, and realized we were so far off from where we told him we were. He might've vanished for good."

"I'm thinking he should have." She swiped her phone open again. "I will now."

"Without Noble, there's no chance, Clarissa. We can't get involved. You know that. We'll be demoted and be on guard duty somewhere in D.C. if this gets out."

She slumped back in her seat. Beck was right. There was no other way. "So what did you tell your CI? He's not gonna hurt Jack, is he?"

"He's not. I told him someone of interest was going to be in town soon. Someone his bosses might be interested in."

"Beck, that's a suicide mission."

"I think it'll draw out whoever else was behind that heist. This is clearly a case of two parties in dispute. One got away with the money. Something tells me my informant is involved with the other party."

"What tells you that? Your gut?"

Beck lifted an eyebrow and said nothing.

"I sure hope you're right, man." Clarissa lifted the bourbon Beck had brought and drained it one pull as she stared out the window, hoping Jack would figure this out quickly.

CHAPTER 4

I STOOD IN THE MIDDLE OF A STREET SURROUNDED BY ROWS OF two-story connected homes on either side running the full length of the road. The driver had let me off a quarter-mile from here. Said he couldn't go into the old section of Bruges. Not sure why. Road was wide enough.

I kept walking until I found the address. A worn stone facade interrupted with splashes of color. A blue door. Red shutters and trim. A post-it note fixed to the door said to knock on the door to the right. I dropped my bags in front of my place, took a few steps down, and rapped on the worn wooden door.

A dog barked. Someone shushed him. Presumably the same someone opened the door and greeted me with a smile. I hadn't thought much about what my contact here would look like, but the gorgeous brunette standing almost eye-to-eye with me wasn't it.

She hesitated a moment before saying, "Hello. You must be Jack?"

I wasn't used to anyone who didn't know me knowing my name. An alias was usually involved. It took me so long to reply she must've begun to think I had knocked on the wrong door.

"Are you?" Her furrowed brows betrayed her smile.

"Sorry, yeah, that's me."

"Great! I'm Katrine. We've been expecting you and are excited to have you staying with us the next four weeks." She leaned to her left, slipping almost entirely out of sight for a few seconds, then returned with a set of keys dangling from a soccer ball keychain. I glanced at her left ring finger. Bare, but only recently. A white line where a ring had been. "These are for you. The silver one opens the front door. Gold, the back door. Skeleton the upstairs, where your master suite is."

She pushed past me and led the way to the next unit. A burst of warmth slipped out of the entryway, carrying with it the smell of brownies.

"It's been so quiet the past few months," she said. "Some years, I'm booked year-round, but not this year."

"Why's that?"

She stopped and looked back and shrugged. "Just the way things go, I guess. Anyway, I started up the heater this morning. There's two units." She pointed at the middle of the wall, then upstairs. "Shouldn't have to mess with them much, as our weather is fairly stable this time of year."

"Cold."

She laughed. "Yes, lots of cold. And rain. But it is still quite nice. Peaceful, you know."

I nodded. "Something smells good."

Her face lit up. "Oh, yes. Come this way."

I followed her into her place and to the kitchen and stayed back a few feet as she bent over in front of the stove and retrieved the pan of brownies.

"Are those magic brownies?" I winked.

"Magic?"

I chuckled. "Pot brownies."

"Oh, marijuana! Um, no, but I can run next door and get you some and a pipe if you—"

I waved her off. "Just making a joke. That won't be necessary."

"Oh." She shrugged. "Well, feel free to stop by any time for some, or a glass of wine, or whatever."

"Might take you up on that."

"Is there a Mrs. Jack?"

"Never had much luck tying down a woman."

"You just need rope, and then you use the right knots."

I didn't know whether to smile or ask her to demonstrate. "What about you? A Mr., uh, I didn't catch your name."

"Katrine." She reached into her pocket and produced a card. "It was in all the email communications."

"Ah, yeah. My assistant handled all of that."

"So, do you run some big company or something like that?"

"Something like that."

"Is this a… what's the word… sabbatical?"

"Something like that."

"Don't like to give much away, do you?"

I grinned. "Something like that."

A silence filled the gap between us as she searched for something else to talk about. Her face tightened, her gaze went to the window, and she flinched when the heat kicked on with a couple bangs.

"Everything OK?" I asked.

She took a breath, shook her head, smiled. "Yes, sorry. Just a little edgy. I don't sleep well some nights, resulting in extra morning coffee. The energy is great, but it makes me jumpy. Come on, let me show you to your place." After giving me the tour, she glanced toward the door a couple of times. "Is there anything else you need in here?"

"No, I won't keep you any longer."

"Well, I'm right next door, and I work from home most days now, so pop on over anytime." She started toward the door to show herself out.

"Katrine, one thing."

She turned, smiling. "Yes?"

"Dinner?"

"I have to make it an early night, but perhaps—"

"Sorry, not like that." I felt a little knot in my stomach as disappointment overtook her smile. "Where's a good place to grab something to eat tonight? Something close. I'd head out to shop, but like you, I'm kinda looking forward to an early night."

"Stores are all closed now anyway. They close at five." She pushed open the door and stepped out, gesturing for me to follow. With a finger aimed down the street, she said, "Go that way and at the end, turn right. Five doors down on the left, go in. He makes something new every night, and it is always delicious."

"Excellent. Get some rest. Maybe I'll bump into you tomorrow."

"You know where to find me, Jack."

CHAPTER 5

THE RESTAURANT KATRINE RECOMMENDED LOOKED LIKE ANY other house on the street. Worn facade that had survived three or four hundred years' worth of wind, rain, snow, and sun. The front door was at least a hundred years old and had been painted over several times, currently sporting a faded red. If not for the open sign dangling from a hook, I'd have figured my host had lied to me.

A strand of bells on the interior side of the door announced my presence as I entered. In front of me, a set of stairs were roped off. A sign written in Dutch presumably said off limits or no entry or something along those lines.

A dining room with four tables spaced evenly led to another doorway, which I figured was the kitchen. A few male voices rose and fell, followed by shared laughter. All along the walls were bottles of wine, beer, and liquor, as well as dozens of photos of people.

"Hello?" I called out.

The genial conversation fell silent, and a tall man with a wide nose and a mop of blond curls appeared in the kitchen doorway. He twisted the corner of his mustache and smiled.

"Serving dinner tonight?" I asked.

"American!"

"Guilty."

"Been so quiet here lately, only locals."

"I bet." I waited a few seconds for an answer. There was none. "Anyway, dinner?"

"Yes, of course, of course. Take a seat wherever you like, and I'll be back in a moment." He disappeared and the door fell shut. His voice rose as he called something out, this time in French. He reappeared with a drink menu and told me tonight's options. All pasta dishes.

"Any chance you got a steak back there?" I asked.

He craned his neck as though he could see into the kitchen through the door. "No, but I do have something I think you'll like."

"As long as its meat, I'm good. And I'll take a beer... uh, a Tripel, whatever you got that's local."

He winked and snapped and hopped off toward the kitchen. A moment later, he returned with my beer. I asked where the restroom was, and he pointed to the far corner. Pushing through the door, I saw a sink on the left, and a urinal on the right. Another door led to a water closet with a full toilet. The setup was interesting, to say the least. Though I'd found that throughout Europe over the years

As I washed my hands, I felt the air suck out of the restroom, and the door banged hard against the frame. I pulled it open, spotted a large man in front of the entrance to the restaurant. He walked over to my table, grabbed my beer.

"Put that down if I was you," I said.

He stopped, arm extended halfway, and looked up at me. "Who the hell are you?" His accent wasn't local, not like Katrine and the restaurant owner. French, maybe? After waiting a moment for my response and not getting it, he said again, "Who the hell are you?"

"Nobody." I crossed the room to the table. We stood opposite each other with the hunk of wood between us. "Just a guy who loves his beer."

"Where's Luc?"

I shrugged. "Who's that?"

He grabbed the top of his head. "The guy with all the curls."

I jutted my chin toward the kitchen, kept my eyes on the guy. "Back there, making my dinner."

The guy set my drink on the table and started toward the back of the room.

"I'd hold off."

He stopped, turned toward me. "Why's that?"

"I'm hungry. Really not a good idea to delay my dinner."

"I think you can wait." He lifted his shirt, showing off his pistol tucked deep into his waistband. Amateur hour. I'd have mine unholstered before he could dig his out of his underwear.

But this wasn't any of my business. So long as he left me alone and didn't delay my dinner too much, I'd stay out of it. I grabbed my beer off the table, offered a half-assed cheers and took a sip.

He didn't figure me much of a threat because he turned his back on me and barreled toward the kitchen, crashing into the swinging door with his shoulder. The door banged so hard against the other side of the wall, I thought it was gonna break off its hinges. But nothing happened after that, not immediately. No raised voices. No fists to faces.

I sat back down and took a few more sips of my beer and waited for a few minutes until my host returned. He came through the door disheveled, a couple buttons missing from his shirt, his hair a mess, his right cheek bright red and his eye swelling.

"Sorry about that," Luc said.

"You need any help back there?"

He stopped, looked down at his shirt, waved me off. "Slipped on a freshly mopped floor is all."

"Accidents happen," I said.

"They sure do."

"Especially when some six-five goon comes in collecting."

Luc looked away, in shame perhaps. "Everyone has got problems, eh?"

"Happens to the best of us, I suppose." I tipped my half-empty glass toward him.

"Another?"

"Sure."

Luc disappeared for a minute and returned with a full glass and a basket of bread. "Ah, wait." He hid the bread behind his back. "You don't eat this, right?"

"Yeah." I took the glass from him and set it on one of the condensation rings on the table. "Luc, you look like a guy that can handle himself."

He made a nonchalant face and shrugged.

"Former military?" I asked.

"Something like that."

"Government work?"

"Maybe." He raised his hand to silence me before I could drill down further. "Why do you ask? Are you the kind of man who has that history as well?"

I leaned back and smiled. "Something like that."

He touched his swollen eye and grimaced. "You know I didn't fall."

"Yeah, I figured. Might want to ice that or throw a steak on it."

He raised a finger and smiled. "No steak. Remember?"

I patted my stomach. "How could I forget?" The room fell silent for a moment. "Look, if you need help with that guy—"

"I wouldn't think of getting someone involved. And you…"

"Jack."

"Jack, well, you should just keep your head down and worry about yourself. Bruges is a wonderful town."

"But?"

"But there's an element here that cares for no one. I'm kind of caught in the middle of something. It's OK, though. We can handle it. Soon it ends and things will go back to normal."

I studied Luc for a moment, wondering what *something* was and what kind of danger he and others in the area might be in.

"I can see it on your face, Jack," he said. "It's really nothing."

"Enough for that goon to pop you in the face."

"I didn't do what I was supposed to do. Simple enough. Won't happen again."

"Luc, I gotta ask, are you part of that group? The element that cares for no one?"

He shook his head. "Just doing what I have to do to make it go away."

"I'm good at that, too. Just so you know. I'm right down the street. Don't hesitate."

He turned toward the kitchen, looked back, said, "I'm gonna close down early tonight. I'll bring you your food to go. Throw in a few bottles of that Tripel, too."

CHAPTER 6

Dylan paced the chilly hotel room from door to window and back again, swinging his head toward the television and watching what little coverage of the Barcelona bombing was on the news. There had been less each day, but he caught every single bit he could. There had been no new leads since they arrested the men in Prague and subsequently released them two days later. They looked nothing like Dylan.

And that was a good thing.

The disguise, simple as it was, had worked. Whatever footage they had of him would never match up. This knowledge eased the knots in his back and stomach. In some ways, it intrigued him he could even feel like that. How many capital crimes had he committed for governments, private groups and citizens, and, well, anyone with enough money to convince him to take someone's life.

He stopped in front of the TV and fell back onto the bed. It was nice having it to himself. Lorraine had become a bit clingy of late, never shutting up about them leaving the life now that they had so much money. No matter how much he reminded her it would be a while before they could live off the money he'd stolen, she didn't listen. He wasn't lying to her, though. A hundred million plus in Bitcoin would take a while to launder through various wallets, bridges, and networks. He had a plan, and once he put it in motion, that money would be split among a hundred wallets in twelve months, then half of it would be deposited into unmarked accounts, which would be further laundered.

In the meantime, they had to be patient, distance themselves from the Barcelona incident, and take whatever jobs came their way to pay the bills.

He glanced over at the nightstand where his phone buzzed. He recognized the number coming through the encrypted messaging and call app and answered the call.

"Yeah, go ahead Luis," he said. Normally, he'd never use names. But the app was unknown to most and created a private tunnel for them to communicate through.

"Hey, Dylan, remember that guy you've been trying to find? The one you missed last year?"

"Noble? My white whale? How could I possibly forget?"

"I think he's here."

"Brussels?"

"Bruges."

"You're kidding me." Dylan pictured the route from Amsterdam to Bruges. He could be there in a few hours. "What's he doing there?"

Luis hesitated a moment. "Hell if I know, boss. We were collecting from one of our clients and he was in there. Tried to get in the way it seemed. Had to put him in his place."

Dylan smirked at the man's lies. Luis was a big guy. Could handle himself well. But he was no match for Noble. As far as Dylan was concerned, a long-range rifle was the best option for Jack.

"How did that go?" Dylan asked, eager to hear the story.

"You know, he just backed off, let us do our thing." He paused a beat and Dylan heard someone in the background. "Yeah, and we watched him leave. Just walked around a bit, but we know the street he's on."

"What makes you so sure he's staying?"

"Just a hunch, I guess."

Dylan rose and walked over to the window where he looked down at the men working the loading dock. "A hunch, huh? Luis, are you keeping something from me?"

"No, and I don't appreciate the accusation. I didn't have to reach out like this. If you don't want our help—"

"Sorry, man. I didn't mean to offend you. We've got a great working relationship, and I don't want to harm or alter that." He turned and leaned back against the window. They only mattered to him until they didn't, and their usefulness had been less than useful lately. "I'll pay you twenty-five thousand to keep an eye on him until I can get down there. Can you do that? If he's out, just, you know, pop in and check up on him. I want him looking out for you guys."

"Twenty-five? Yeah we can do that. And if you can't get down here, just bump that up to a cool hundred thousand and we can do the job for you."

"We'll see if it comes to that, Luis. But, as of right now, Noble is mine."

CHAPTER 7

THE SOUND OF A CHILD'S LAUGHTER WHISPERED IN MY EAR. "Mia," I muttered as shades of reality intertwined with that subconscious swirl of firing neurons that is sleep. I blinked open my eyes and scanned the unfamiliar room. I called for my daughter again. Hope faded by the second as my situation became clearer.

Mia was nowhere near here. In fact, her location was unknown. But I knew where I was. Belgium, near the coast, in a quaint town called Bruges.

I sat up in bed, stretched out my legs, arms, back. Kicking my feet over the edge, I heard the laughter again. It was coming from the cracked window behind the bed, on the back wall. Behind the unit was a shared backyard with the one next door. Katrine's place. And there she was, tossing a ball to a little girl maybe three or four years old who whiffed badly on each throw.

I staggered across the room and down the stairs. My limp lessened and joints loosened. By the time I reached the back door, I felt mostly human.

The little girl turned and smiled as though I was her best friend as I pulled the door open and stepped into the small garden.

"Oh, I hope we didn't wake you," Katrine said, crouched at the far end of the patio.

"No, not at all. Was up reading." I turned my attention to the little one. "What's your name?"

"I'm Bernie." Her smile beamed.

"She knows English already?" I was surprised.

Katrine nodded. "Started her right away. Isn't that right, Bernadette?"

The little girl nodded.

"How old? Three?"

Katrine rose from her crouching position. "That's right. And if you'll watch her a moment, I'll grab you a coffee." She hurried into her house before I could tell her yes.

Bernie took a few steps closer and attempted to throw the ball to me. Of course, I made a big deal of how well she threw it.

"You know, I have a little girl, too."

"What's her name?" Bernie's voice sounded like a series of squeaks that somehow made sense.

"Mia."

Her eyes grew wide. "Oooh, I have a friend name Mia."

"I bet she's a feisty one."

Bernie looked confused and averted her attention to the ball again. With her eyes aimed at the ground, she spoke up again. "Do you know where my dad is?" Her eyes misted over as she looked up at me. "Are you his friend?"

I looked toward the door, Katrine wasn't in sight. "Afraid not, sweetie. I've only just met your mother. What's his name?"

"Daddy." She looked so innocent while giving her reply.

"When was the last time you saw him?"

She clasped her hands behind her back and teetered side-to-side. "I... don't remember."

"Oh, boy," Katrine said as she hurried toward us. Coffee spilled over the rim of the mug. "I'm sorry about that. Didn't expect her to, um, how's that phrase go? Air our dirty laundry?"

"She was asking about—"

"Her father." She picked her daughter up and held her on her hip. "Let me get her settled inside, and I'll explain."

The quiet overtook the small area like fog rolling in, and for a moment everything that had happened and was to happen didn't matter. The air was still, cool, but not cold, and offered a hint of winter weather to come. The sun shone through silvery wisps of clouds that bunched and blackened to the west.

The coffee was strong, perked me up. It took less than two minutes to down the European-size mug though, and it wasn't nearly enough to make me a functioning member of society. I considered going in to pour another cup but thought better of it. Didn't want Katrine to get the wrong idea.

I pictured her little girl's eyes as she asked if I knew her father. Wondered if Mia had asked that question of others, if her eyes had filled with tears threatening to break past her lids like water cresting the top of a dam.

The reality that Mia was better off with my brother, who was already raising a family, weighed heavy on me. All I could offer her was a few weeks before my old life—which was supposed to have been shredded so I could move on—caught up to me.

"And I'm back." Katrine emerged with a smile on her face, a carafe in her right hand, and a plate of pastries in her left. "Figured you'd like some more coffee. I know you Americans like to drink giant-size portions of the stuff." She set the carafe on a stained-glass bistro table and extended the plate to me. "Pastry?"

"Don't do carbs," I said. "But I'll definitely help myself to some American-size servings of coffee."

Katrine looked me up and down. "I thought people cut carbs to lose weight. You look pretty fit."

"Energy."

"Energy?"

"Feel weighed down, sluggish, tired when I eat bread and crap. Give me two or three steaks a day, I never run out of energy."

"Weird."

"Guess so."

"I couldn't live without pastries."

"We've all got our thing."

She didn't speak for the next few minutes, allowing me time to finish two more small cups of coffee.

"Pretty good stuff," I said. "Local roaster?"

She shrugged. "Just something I get from the store. Your daughter's name is Mia?"

"Yeah. She's a little firecracker. I don't get to see her much. Miss her."

"Is that due to your travel?"

"Something like that. I wasn't told about her when she was born. Didn't find out for a few years. I've tried to be as present as I can. We were vacationing for a few months in the Florida Keys when I got called to come out here."

"That must be hard to deal with."

I nodded. "Not something I can really put into words."

"I understand that. I have something like that myself." After a few more minutes, she spoke again. "My husband disappeared three months ago. He went out to meet some friends for dinner and a few beers and never came home."

"Sorry to hear that."

"It's not your fault." She took a deep breath and exhaled, then continued. "Things weren't perfect between us, hadn't been in some time. We thought having Bernie would help us grow close again, but the past three years were worse than the previous four. We should've ended it."

I waited for her to continue, but she sulked into a chair and looked up at the darkening sky. "Did his friends have any information? Like, when he left? Did he leave with one of them? Someone else…?"

She glanced at me, confirming my suspicion that the "friends" he went to meet was actually a woman.

"How long had he been seeing her?" I asked.

She glanced toward the ground, back up at the sky, and let her gaze fall on me. "I'm not sure. I didn't know about her until afterward. It wasn't unusual for him to be out late when he went out with his friends, so when eleven arrived, I went upstairs to bed. I woke up to the sun, and he still wasn't home."

"Did that ever happen before?"

"Not without a message and a photo showing me he was with his pals."

"No message this time, I presume."

"That's right. No message." She poured herself a coffee. "I called his best friend who said they were out, but he left early, as did a few of the other guys."

"So he was with his friends?"

"For a while, yes. And none of them would tell me the entire truth that morning. It wasn't until nighttime fell and he still hadn't returned."

"Then one of them spilled about his mistress?"

Katrine shook her head as she took a sip of coffee. "No, I followed Cort —his best friend since childhood—that afternoon. All the way across town where it isn't so nice as it is here."

She didn't have to paint much of a picture. "You found Cort talking with his mistress."

"In a bar, yes. Of course, I didn't know it was Nev's mistress. I thought Cort was screwing around on his wife."

"What'd you do?"

A sorrowful smile formed. "I waited for him to come out and confronted him. Asked him how he could be with a woman when his best friend has been missing for a day. And how could he do this to his wife." The smile faded and her expression grew dark. "Immediately his hands went up, and he said I had it wrong. He backed up, opened the door, and called the woman out."

I said nothing while she collected herself and wiped tears from her eyes.

"The rest of it blurs, honestly. His words. Expression. Her face as she realized she stood face-to-face with Nev's wife. And then she admitted they were together the night before, as they had been at least twice a week for the past year." The tears came hard now. "And you know, I don't give a single fuck about that, Jack. I could take him or leave him at this point. Bernie was, and is, most important, and I wanted her to grow up in a family. But now? Had he turned up...if he ever turns up, we are finished."

"Do you want him to turn up again?" I asked.

She shook her head. "No, I don't. But for my daughter's sake, yeah, I wish he would."

"So, the mistress. What else did she say?"

"That Nev left around one in the morning. She didn't hear from him after."

"Katrine, my background is complicated, to say the least. But finding people who don't want to be found, or can't be found, is something I have experience with. I can help you."

Her face steeled. "I can't ask you to do that."

"You don't have to ask. I'm offering." I wanted to stop myself. The hell was I doing trying to be a hero again? I had no skin in this game.

"Jack, believe me, you don't want to get involved. Some things are better left undisturbed. If he's out there, and wants to come back, he will."

"Look, it's really not—"

"I have to go now. You can see yourself home."

CHAPTER 8

LATER THAT AFTERNOON, I SET OFF TO CHECK OUT A LOCAL Trappist brewery that had been in operation for over four hundred years. They'd adhered to the same recipe the entire time. Next was a torture museum. Found a few exhibits that I'd lived through. I topped it off with a visit to a chocolate museum. Figuring that was enough of playing tourist for the next three years, I found myself at home in a dive bar.

It wasn't as seedy as what I might find in a back alley in New York, but it'd do. The cast of characters seated around the bar told me this was an establishment that did not thrive on tourist dollars.

I figured these weren't the type of folks who'd be chatty with the guy from the States, so I opted for the right end of the bar where there were four empty stools. I sat in the last. It took the bartender half a second to recognize I wasn't from around there. He walked up and spoke English to me. I ordered a burger and a bourbon and excused myself to the bathroom, which wasn't quite the experience it was at Luc's establishment.

The air in the bar felt heavier as I exited the restroom. Sure, the smell of the grill and beer and booze mixed to offer a subtle reminder of New Orleans in the summer, but something was off. The chatter had died. The music silenced.

The big guy from the previous night at Luc's was sitting two stools down from my spot. Another guy, much shorter, was parked next to him.

They both stared me down as I took my seat. I offered nothing to them, not even a nod. I grabbed my bourbon and downed it in one swig, then called for another and a beer.

After my food arrived, and I'd eaten half the burger, the big guy spoke up.

"Where do I know you from?"

Not much recall there, I figured. Too many hits to the head.

"You don't." I took another bite and washed it down with beer.

"I definitely know you." He nudged his buddy in the ribs. "Something about his face, isn't there?"

The shorter guy said, "It's a punchable face." They shared a laugh, and the second guy got up, rounded the big dude, and took the stool next to me.

I didn't budge. Took another bite. Another swig of beer.

"Why's your face so punchable?" he said, loud enough for everyone at the bar to hear.

Over the years, I'd developed the ability to read people's expressions without looking directly at them. Everyone's face was saying, "Ah shit, the American is about to get pummeled."

"You hear me, you muppet? Tell me, why is your face so damn punchable?" He had his right foot on the ground, left perched on the bottom stool support. At any moment, he could pivot hard and try to crash down on my face with a left hook.

"Maybe it's because I look like the guy your mom ran off with. Try calling me daddy. See how it feels."

His face hardened. A strike was imminent. Then I saw a large hand clasp his shoulder, and his expression softened. It was as though his larger friend was saying, "Not in here, pal."

"You're a funny guy, yeah?" he said to me.

"Most people would say no. But, yeah, I agree with you."

"You won't be so funny with no teeth."

I pushed my plate toward the bartender, who was hovering nearby, one hand hidden under his apron, gripping a weapon of some sort. I held up my hand to indicate it'd be OK.

"I stopped in to have some dinner and a few drinks. Not take out the garbage. But if that's what I gotta do—" I slid off my stool, kept my back to the wall, squared up with the guy, "—then I'm glad to pitch in so these folks can enjoy their liquid dinners."

The short guy puffed up his chest, clenched his fists. His eyes betrayed him. Behind the hardened, stubbled face, was fear, and it shone through his eyes.

I bared my teeth. "Come on, take a swing. See how many of these pearly whites you can knock out."

He started bouncing on his toes, like a prize fighter waiting for the bell to ding so he could charge his opponent with the ferocity of a raging bull. A sheen of sweat coated his forehead. He worked his fingers out, back into a fist, out again.

"Stop delaying, *muppet*."

That was apparently enough to tip him over the edge. He reared back and swung at me. It was a terrible, looping motion, like he thought he was maximizing torque, but was using all shoulder instead of driving with his hips.

It was an easy blow to deflect. I leaned back. Grabbed his wrist and elbow. Guided him into the bar, which he struck with all his momentum squarely in the solar plexus. His breath escaped in a ghoulish exhale. He grasped at the counter, but with his knees buckling, couldn't find a hand-hold and collapsed to the floor, holding his stomach.

As easy as he was to take out, I knew the big guy would be a much tougher fight, and this room was not where I wanted to take him on. A guy like that can cover a lot of ground in a few steps. And there wasn't much space to maneuver in there.

He took a deep breath, stood, shook his head. "Hotheads, right?"

I nodded while anticipating his next move. It surprised me.

He pulled out a wad of cash, dropped several bills on the bar. Then he grabbed his buddy by the collar and dragged him to his feet. "What did I say? In and out. Nice and easy." He cocked back and slapped the guy across the face. The short man winced, held up his hand to protect himself. The big guy shoved him toward the exit. "Good. Good. Now go wait by the door."

The guy shuffled off, glancing back once at me before continuing his walk of shame.

The big guy turned to me. "Last night at Luc's place. That's where I saw you."

I nodded.

"And now, I come to visit another of my clients, and here you are again."

"The world is full of crazy coincidences."

"Two is a coincidence, right?"

I nodded again.

"Then three times would be a pattern. And if I notice a pattern developing, I have to make sure it doesn't continue."

I said nothing during his grand pause meant to intimidate me.

"Do we have an understanding?"

"Sure."

"Good."

"We run into each other again, I'm gonna have to do to you what I did to him." I gestured to his buddy by the door. "And I can. And I will."

I could feel the tension build in the room. They all knew who this guy was. They all feared him and anyone associated with him. Other than his size, he had nothing. Which meant whoever was behind him held the power. Who was that?

His scowl evaporated into a smile. "You don't know me."

"You're wrong, pal. You're the same as every other overgrown goon I've ever encountered. Think your size and a pistol are all you need to get whatever you want. You're nothing but a bully, and I've never let a bully walk all over me."

"You couldn't be more wrong." With that, he turned and left the bar.

CHAPTER 9

I TOOK MY TIME FINISHING THE REST OF MY BURGER, KEENLY aware of the bartender's stare burning a hole through my chest. With a couple bites left, I set my knife and fork down and looked over at him.

"Help you, friend?"

"You ain't my friend, mate." His rough Irish accent sounded out of place. "And you ain't doin' no one here no favors actin' a tough guy."

"Not sure what the problem is. Couple of goons tried to press on me, and I stood up for myself. That's not allowed in these parts? Just supposed to roll over and let them have their way?"

The bartender shook his head. Flops of red curls bounced. "You should just watch your back, 'specially if that's your second run-in with 'em."

"Just the big guy."

"He's the one you needing to be worried about."

My interest was piqued. "Who is he, anyway?"

"Someone you shouldn't trifle with."

"That's not much help."

"That's all you need to know." He turned his back on me and grabbed a rack of dirty mugs. "And you'd be wise to listen to what I'm saying. Let it soak in. Absorb it."

"Who's he work for?"

The bartender set the rack on the counter and walked over. His voice hushed, he said, "Are you stupid, mate? These guys will string you up by your pecker, cut off your bollocks, and force feed them to you. You'll be lucky if you choke to death on them, 'cause if you don't, they'll cut off your fingers, one at a time, then your toes—"

"Then my nose, dick, and whatever else is left. Yeah, I got it."

The bartender shook his head, looked down. "The hell is wrong with you, mate? Look, my advice to you is get the hell out of town. You're on their radar, and that's not a good place to be. Cut your vacation short, whatever you gotta do. Just get outta here."

"Never been one to take advice that says to cut and run. I've done nothing wrong here. No reason for them to keep harassing me."

"Then it's your funeral, mate." He chuckled and turned away again.

"Wait." I paused long enough for him to look back. "Give me a name. Let me check things out. Maybe I can help out here."

"What don't you get? There's nothing to help out with. We have a system and, sure, it's flawed, but it works. Got that? It just works. The owner keeps his bar. I keep my job. It's that way up and down the streets here in Bruges. So, I strongly encourage you to get the hell outta this town before you mess things up for the rest of us. Because if proprietors start losing their businesses, and people like me start losing their jobs, it ain't just the *goons* you'll be worrying about."

By this point, all eyes were on me. Around the room, they cursed me under their breath, while hatred filled their eyes. What had I done, other than defend myself?

"Can see that anyone with a spine isn't welcome in here." I reached into my pocket and pulled out a wad of cash, dropped it on the bar, finished my beer. "Anyone wants to fill me in, I'm sure you all can figure out where to find me."

Thirty seconds later, I'd covered a block and a half with someone following for at least half the time. They made little effort to conceal their stalking. Didn't even silence their phone's camera shutter sound.

I walked at a moderate clip, checking window reflections in my peripheral every so often to keep tabs on my tail. They maintained their distance but were creeping up on me. After a few more blocks, I ducked into a small grocery store, positioned myself behind a display and waited.

The woman who entered was not what I had been expecting. I only knew it was her by her red wool coat. She had long blonde hair, pulled back in a tight ponytail. She was on the taller end of medium height and had a slender but athletic build.

She scanned the store, her gaze passing right over my location. For a few minutes she remained near the entrance. A couple of people entered and had to squeeze past her. She refused to move. Finally, an employee walked over to speak with her. She ignored them, turning her attention to her cell phone.

A message or call?

A picture of me?

She shook her head, tucked the phone in her pocket, glanced around the store again. The employee spoke louder now. She engaged him, pointing her finger in his face. His cheeks burned red. He backed off.

Then she left.

But not before I snapped a picture of her. Figured I'd try to load it up on Google and see if any matches came back. If that didn't work, I still had a contact or two who might be able to help.

A breathy laugh escaped my mouth. Was I really acting this paranoid? For what? A cute blonde who may have been tailing me? But then, given what else had happened in my short time in town, perhaps I was right being on guard.

I let a minute pass before stepping out from behind my cover. She hadn't returned, and I had shopping to do.

With a couple of full bags of groceries, I made my way back to the rental. The setting sun cast the buildings in an orange then pink and purple wash. I paused to study the changing sky, taking it in. Wasn't often I took moments like this to breathe. To stop thinking. To find some peace.

Peace.

What a crock.

The last traces of color were fading behind the row of homes as I made my final turn. Another minute, I'd be home.

Footsteps rose from behind, hurried, slapping the cobblestone, echoing off the buildings. I glanced over my shoulder. Saw someone approaching.

By the time I turned around, she was five feet from me, cell phone in one hand, pistol in the other, tight to her leg.

The blonde from earlier, minus the red coat. Had she wanted me to see her? Had it been a coincidence she ran into me? Whatever the reason, she had managed to track me back to the rental, which called into question whether she had been onto me from the moment I arrived in Bruges.

She held her ground but wasn't close enough for me to reach. Even if she was, I'd have to drop the bags, which would be a dead giveaway I was about to attack. All she'd have to do is flick her wrist upward and squeeze the trigger. That would take less time than for me to throw a punch.

Her piercing blue eyes stood out even in the shadows. Her breath vaporized in front of her face, rising like smoke and dissipating into the darkening sky.

"Help you?" I said, in part to buy time, and also because I was genuinely curious why this woman had followed me for more than two miles.

She lifted her pistol a few inches, kept it aimed at the ground between us. After a deep breath, she said, "Who are you, and why are you getting in the middle of my investigation?"

CHAPTER 10

LORRAINE HAD NEVER CARED FOR MUCH OF ANYTHING WHILE growing up. She knew that made her odd. While her friends had this favorite band or that passion they couldn't stop talking about, all she wanted to do was exist. Soon enough, while they all moved on, all Lorraine did was exist. Nothing mattered. She thought that made her special. Like a monk.

Or something.

It wasn't until she *agreed* to therapy as part of a court-ordered mandate following a brutal assault on an ex-boyfriend who thought it was OK to beat her, that she realized she wasn't stoic.

"You are apathetic and a sociopath."

The first four or five sessions, she wore headphones. Even had music playing the first couple of times. Then she listened to nothing. Just pretended by tapping along to a fake beat. For his part, her therapist, Ron, said nothing. He stared at the notebook in his lap and spent the session doodling.

Or something.

Then Lorraine spoke. And after a little back and forth with Ron, the faucet turned on and everything she had ever held in rushed out. Every shitty thing she had ever done to herself, her family, friends, random people. She became aware of how terrible a person she was.

Initially, she attempted to make amends.

But then, one day following her session with Ron, she met *him*.

He had been waiting outside. Lorraine nearly tripped when he spoke to her. She wasn't ugly, but she wouldn't win any beauty contests. Not that it mattered. She was content being average and overlooked most of the time.

He, on the other hand, could've been a Greek god sent down from Mount Olympus. His only purpose being to devastate her. Dark brown hair that sat perfectly. A strong jaw and chin, coated in stubble. Eyes that made her knees weak every time he stared intently at her over the course of the following month.

She started ditching her therapy sessions to spend time with him. Not a good idea, as the therapy was court-mandated. If her attendance dropped below a certain threshold, a warrant for her arrest would be issued. She was teetering dangerously close to that line. And she didn't care. All the therapy in the world couldn't provide the clarity he had. He helped her understand herself. Why make amends for shit that happened because of how you were wired?

It made sense. So much so that she questioned nothing in those early days. It all seemed so coincidental that he had appeared in her life, so ready and willing to sweep her off her feet and carry her away.

And he had.

He offered Lorraine a chance to escape from that shithole apartment in Paris. He took her to Amsterdam, provided a life where money did not matter anymore. She could buy anything, do anything, be anything she ever wanted. With him, she no longer felt apathetic. She engaged with the world in a way she never had.

For the first year, their relationship had been amazing. She couldn't remember life before him. Couldn't imagine life without him. But slowly, things changed. His business trips lasted longer. The details grew shadier. He concealed information from her, things like his destination and even the reason for traveling.

Eventually, her cynicism and distrust returned, and she questioned him.

"Where are you going this time?"

"You know I'm not going to answer that," he had said.

"I can't keep doing this with you."

"You like the money, right? The lifestyle? It has to come from somewhere."

"I don't care about that. I miss you. I worry about you. What if something happens? I have no way of even knowing."

He had smiled at her response. "Now I know you're ready."

She realized at that moment he had been grooming her. For what, she had wondered. It didn't take long to find out. To learn that the man she had fallen in love with was nothing but a criminal. That he'd been in court that day and spotted her. Followed her after. The internal struggle that went along with coming to grips with this newfound knowledge would have been enough to drive most women away.

Lorraine was not most women.

Her passion renewed, knowing he was out doing whatever it took to build their life. And she wanted to join him.

So, she did.

"How much longer do we have to stay here?" Lorraine stood at the window, staring out at the abysmal view of the hotel's loading dock. Workers stood around, smoking cigarettes and drinking from flasks. "With all that money, we should be able to abandon all of this, Dylan."

He crossed the room and stood behind her, his hands on her hips, his breath on her neck. "It's not that easy. We have to move the Bitcoin around and launder it some. Plus, I want the rest. So, we're gonna stay a little while longer. We need to make sure there's no evidence of me being within a hundred miles of that building. Besides, I have an unfinished job I must complete before retiring."

"Just let that go."

"I can't, and you know that. We almost had him in Luxembourg. He'll make another mistake again soon."

"When will we know that you're in the clear for the bombing?"

"My guy in DSGE is keeping me posted on all available and related intel. Though he's with the French government, he's got strong connections in Spain. Some days, the news is good. Other days, not so much."

He gripped her waist tighter, indicating an increase in stress or anxiety.

"What's the latest news?" Lorraine asked.

He took a deep breath. His exhale was hot against her exposed neck. She hadn't been happy to cut off her hair and dye it red but understood why the change had been necessary. It wasn't every day your boyfriend blew up a building and stole a hundred million dollars. The following few days had been stressful, but soon she knew it would pass.

"The body count doesn't match," he said. "The hope is they'll believe the difference is just due to the explosion, but investigators are questioning why they can't account for all missing and presumed victims."

She spun in a half-circle and let her bare back come to rest on the cold glass window. He leaned in to kiss her. She turned her head, and instead he was stuck with a mouthful of her hair.

"Is there any reason why bodies should be missing?" She avoided his gaze. Over the past two years, she'd learned all his tells. This was one time she didn't want to know if he was lying. "This was simply a distraction, right?"

He released her hips and took a half-step back. "You know it is better you don't ask questions."

"I know, but this is so different from any other operations we've conducted. I'm trying to make sense of it, is all."

"When it's all said and done, we'll be swimming in so much money, it won't matter who, what, why, how."

"And when."

"What?"

"You already said what. I was just filling in the when."

He grinned at her facetiousness. "Right, all of that. Trust me. The payoff is almost here. It is so close, I can taste the piña coladas we'll be sipping down in the Canary Islands."

"Promise?"

"Have I ever lied?"

She rolled her eyes.

"About anything important," he said.

She rolled her eyes again.

"You don't trust me now?"

"Of course I do. I'm just scared. Or bored. Or both. I feel like I should be more involved in this."

"There's nothing to be involved in for at least a few hours." He stepped in closer and hooked his thumbs into her waistband. "Now maybe we should get you out of these shorts."

CHAPTER 11

I WAS HALF A BLOCK FROM MY RENTAL AND QUESTIONED whether I'd ever get there. The woman standing across from me inched her pistol higher every few seconds I remained silent. The wind had switched, and now came in harsh, heavy, and cold. Her hair whipped about in the gusts.

All my senses were heightened. The cold found its way through the loose knit of my sweater. The smell of grill smoke, maybe from Luc's, permeated the air. Chatter from any of the townhomes along the street rose and fell, sometimes followed by laughter. Sometimes by shouts.

I heard, felt, smelled it all. But I only saw the woman across from me, who now pointed her firearm at my gut.

I had nothing to say in response to her question.

"I don't like to repeat myself," she said. "Who are you? Why are you interfering with my investigation?"

I tried to make myself look the least threatening as possible and placed my hands in view. "I'm nobody. Just here on vacation."

"Then why were those men so interested in you?"

"Ran into the big guy at a restaurant last night."

"Which one?"

I gestured behind me. "Neighborhood place. Back there."

"What was your interaction with him?"

I shook my head. "I barely remember him. Was too focused on my food."

"How long have you been here?"

"Not even two days."

"You always make friends this fast?"

"If by friends you mean enemies, then yeah. Faster, usually."

"What's your name?" She lowered the pistol an inch. It didn't comfort me, as it was now aimed at my crotch.

"Again, I'm nobody. I'm not here to interfere in whatever you've got going on with those guys."

"I've got nothing going on with them. And you still haven't answered my question."

"Jack. That's my name."

"Just Jack?"

"What does it matter, lady?"

"Where are you staying?"

"All right," I said. "I'm done with this. You wanna shoot me, go ahead. But I'm done playing twenty questions with you."

Her mouth hung open. She wasn't used to someone blowing her off, especially when she held them at gunpoint. She lowered the pistol until it aimed at her foot.

"See ya around."

I turned and walked toward my rental. Every instinct told me to keep going past it, but for some reason, when I reached the door, I stopped, pulled out my keys and unlocked it. When I turned my head to see if she had followed me, the street was empty. Perhaps she'd watched me until I reached the door. Maybe she was staying close by or had found a cranny somewhere to hide herself and was still watching. It didn't matter. I didn't care. If she showed up, whether alone or with a couple of goons of her own, I'd deal with the situation then.

After entering the rental, I closed the back windows and turned the heat up. Then I put on some coffee and took a seat on the couch after it finished brewing. From there, I did nothing but drink a couple of cups and let my mind wander to no place in particular.

A knock on the door roused me from my meditative state. I answered, expecting the two goons to be there wearing matching brass knuckles. Seeing Katrine standing there holding a bottle of wine and a foil-covered platter was a pleasant surprise.

"Sorry to come over unannounced." She squeezed through the opening, past me, and headed for the kitchen. "Bernie went home with her grandmother this afternoon, so I thought we could have dinner together."

"There's a bottle opener… somewhere, I guess."

Katrine laughed. It was light, airy. Sounded like a young girl's laugh. Not a woman, mother, wife, whose husband was missing. Had she been drinking?

"Guess you know where things are in here," I said.

She looked up and smiled. "Yeah, I kinda outfitted and decorated the place." She reached up and pulled down two wine glasses and filled each about halfway. "Come on. Come drink."

I met her at the island separating the living room and kitchen. She stood on the other side, peeling the foil off the platter.

"Smells good." I hoisted my glass, and she met it with hers. "Cheers."

"Cheers. A roast. Had it slow-cooking all day." She licked the juice from her fingers. Whether she meant to entice me, she certainly had. She caught me staring and smiled again. "It's so good."

"Yeah, I bet." I grabbed a couple plates and silverware and set them on the island so she could serve us. "Hey, you didn't see anyone odd out there when you came over, did you?"

She slowly cut through the meat and kept her eyes down. "Odd? Like how? Did something happen today?" Her voice was tight.

"Couple of out-of-place guys. One big, the other not quite as big. A blonde woman, about your height, maybe hanging around down the block."

She set the knife down and placed a thick slice of roast on each plate, then slid one in my direction. "Just what did you do today, Jack?"

I chuckled. "Only stopped off for a beer."

"You the kind of guy who finds trouble wherever he goes?"

"Sure seems that way."

"Can't say I saw anyone who fit those descriptions. I do have a camera doorbell thing, though. We can check."

"Maybe later. Let's eat."

Half an hour later, we'd finished dinner and half the bottle of wine. Small talk only carried us so far. We sat in silence until our glasses were empty, then she refilled them. I followed her back to the kitchen.

"Why are you here?" I asked.

She set the bottle on the counter and looked up at me with wet eyes.

"What's going on?" I asked

"I was thinking about what you said earlier." She bit her bottom lip as her gaze bounced around the room before settling on me. "About helping me to find Nev?"

"Happy to help. I can go shake a few branches and see what falls out."

"You'd really do that?"

"Katrine, I said I'd help. And I will. But I need you to be honest with me."

"Of course. I can tell you his friends, places he liked to visit, even what I know about his mistress."

"Right, but not just that."

"What else?"

"What's going on around here?"

"What do you mean?"

"I went to Luc's for dinner last night, and while there, some big goon comes in. I couldn't see what happened in the kitchen, but it sure seemed like he was there to shake Luc down." I paused for a beat. "Then today, I run into the same guy a few miles away from here in a bar. He wasn't alone this time, and his little buddy got aggressive with me."

"Did they hurt you?" She reached across the counter for my face.

I leaned back. "No, I'm not the one who left hurting. But what are the odds I'm around that guy twice in less than twenty-four hours? Who is he? Is he following me? What's going on here?"

"Some local thugs acting as enforcers and collectors for someone else."

"Who's this someone else?"

"I couldn't tell you because I'm smart enough not to get involved."

"Was your husband smart enough to not get involved?"

She bent over and pulled another bottle of wine from under the sink. I gave her a look and she shrugged it off. "Never know when you need a spare bottle." She uncorked it and topped off our glasses. "You should follow my lead."

I picked up my glass. "We're neck and neck far as I can tell."

She rolled her eyes. "Not the wine, idiot. Being smart about those men. Don't get involved, Jack. It's not worth it. What they can do to you. To the people you're trying to help. You'll only make it worse. And then if you manage to get them to back off, the organization will just send a few new thugs to take over."

"Organization?"

Her lips thinned, and she looked away. She realized she had said too much.

"So, it's not just someone else. It's a group."

"Don't get involved, Jack. Believe me." A tear crested her eyelid and rolled down her cheek.

"You never told me what you or your husband did for work."

She looked down and swirled her glass on the counter. Wine rose up and nearly spilled over the rim. She stayed silent.

"You tell me not to get involved with them. At the same time, I believe you think these guys have something to do with Nev's disappearance."

"We owned a florist shop." She looked up, forced a smile. "Imagine me, selling tulips all day." Her face turned grim. "It was a few years ago when they started showing up, demanding things. Money, mostly. Sometimes they'd want twenty percent of one of our shipments, only to destroy it in front of us."

"Why?"

"Why not?" Her eyelids fluttered as she shook her head. "After nearly a decade of running a profitable business, we were forced to shut down within sixteen months of the start of the harassment. All because of these assholes."

"That's terrible. What did you do afterward? Go to the police?"

She laughed at that. "The police? Are you kidding. They're no match. And besides, they are likely paid off by... Anyway, it was seven months ago. Now I work part time for a greenhouse nursery, and I help out at Bernie's preschool when I can." She waved her hand in the air. "Outside of the past few months, this place is rented most of the time and provides a decent income. I own the units outright. These belonged to my parents, who left them to me when they passed."

"Sorry to hear that."

Katrine shrugged and cast her eyes down. "These things happen, and fortunately, I have a wonderful mother-in-law who treats me as her own daughter."

"And your husband? What did he do?"

"Same as he did before. Nothing." Her face tightened. "Well, that's not entirely true."

"How so?"

"His whole life with me, he mooched off me. The money I inherited? He lost half of it, gambling, taking his friends out, sometimes on vacations. I resented him, but he did nothing for so long, and I accepted it. Finally, I put my foot down. He only got an allowance. I had hoped that would make him behave."

"No such luck." Didn't take too far of a walk to realize the guy wouldn't change his ways.

She sighed. "What can you do? One day, I hear he got into it with one of those guys you were asking about. Tried to attack him from behind. It didn't go so well for him. Nearly ended up in the hospital. He got better, but the run-ins continued more frequently, and not at his instigation. Before, these guys were only doing their jobs. But now, it was personal to them."

"What does your gut say? They have something to do with his disappearance?"

"It wouldn't take much to connect those dots. But I can't explain why, I don't think they are involved. I think my husband ran like the coward he is."

"Where would he have—"

We both turned toward the banging on the front door.

CHAPTER 12

KATRINE ROUNDED THE ISLAND AND HEADED TOWARD THE door. The incessant banging must've sparked some fear in her that whoever was out there had news. About her husband. Kid. Her mother-in-law. Who knew what was going through her mind?

I hurried across the room and stopped her. She began protesting. I put my finger to her lips and mouthed for her to stay quiet. Her wild eyes settled on mine. I felt a rush of warm air over my hand as she exhaled deeply.

"Are you expecting someone?" she whispered.

I shook my head, then pointed toward the kitchen. She understood my meaning and ten seconds later had armed herself with a knife and taken refuge behind the counter. With her out of sight, I retrieved the 9mm I had tucked in my waistband.

Another round of banging, faster, louder. I peeled back the curtain an inch. That didn't offer enough field of view to see who was out there. What if it was the guys from earlier? A bar with witnesses was one thing. The big man had exercised some restraint there. A brawl with them in the close quarters of the house wouldn't have that same luxury. They'd come in armed with some sort of weapon, meaning I'd have no choice but to shoot, which undoubtedly would bring with it extra scrutiny from law enforcement leading to my face being plastered all over the news. There were plenty of people I didn't want to see that.

But what if it was someone for Katrine? Someone with some information she needed. Or a person in danger. They saw the light on and took a chance.

A long pause ensued. There was no noise beyond the door. Finally, after thirty seconds or so, another round of knocks rose. But this time they were softer, faster.

"Who is it?"

"Open the door," a woman said. "We have to hurry."

One look at Katrine's expression, and I knew she recognized the voice. As the recollection set in, she sprang into action, hurrying from the kitchen to the door. Shoving me out of the way. I grabbed her arm, signaled for her to wait. She threw up her hands.

"It's OK," she said.

"I just want to be ready for anything."

Shaking her head, she pulled the door open. The woman standing outside had tears in her eyes. She clutched the lapel of her coat with both hands so tight her fingers were white. Whatever came next would not be good news.

Katrine backed up and gestured for the woman to enter, which she did, rushing toward Katrine and throwing her arms around her.

"I'm so sorry." She repeated it a half-dozen times.

Katrine peeled the woman off. "What happened?" Panic set in. "Did something happen to Bernie?"

"No, no."

"My mother-in-law?"

"You haven't heard yet?" She took Katrine's hand and led her to the couch.

"Just tell me Bernie is OK."

"They are OK."

"Then what is it?"

"Nev."

Katrine straightened at hearing her husband's name. "Nev?" She pulled away from the other woman. "Is he back?"

Her friend wiped away a new spate of tears and shook her head. "They recovered his body."

Katrine stood and crossed the room. Her head ticked side-to-side as she processed the information. "He...he's dead?"

Her friend nodded, closed the gap between them, put her hand on Katrine's.

Katrine looked up from the floor. Her eyes were red, wet. "Was he found nearby?"

The other woman's face drew tight. "No, he was identified among the rubble of that apartment building explosion in Barcelona. He was in one of the apartments that were obliterated."

"Barcelona?" Katrine's eyebrows knit together. Her eyes darted from one end of the room to the other. "Barcelona?" she repeated.

"Yes."

"That's more than twelve hours from here. As far as I know, he hasn't been there in years. Had he been there for the past three months? Why? What was he doing there?"

Their conversation faded as my mind raced to put together puzzle pieces. I found myself in the middle of a missing person's case that somehow turned into even more of a mystery. I had half a mind to send Clarissa a text thanking her. Then again, she and Beck specifically wanted me here. Did they know all of this and that's why I was in Bruges?

"Will I need to go there? To identify him?" Katrine had lost all color and in the midst of processing this news, appeared ten years older.

"I asked this, and they said we would only need to go to the local police station. There was enough identifying information found with him."

"We?" I interrupted. "I understand why Katrine would need to go, but why you?"

Katrine reached out toward me. "Sorry, Jack. This is Noelle, Nev's sister."

Then it made sense. Next of kin was notified. Perhaps they had called next door while Katrine was here with me.

"Your mother is supposed to be back with Bernie soon," Katrine said.

"She's going to be devastated. Maybe we should go get Bernie and not tell Mom?"

"That's not necessary. She's likely close to sleeping. She can stay there, and we'll break the news in the morning." Then she took a moment to wipe the tears from her face and centered herself with a couple of deep breaths. "Would you come with me, Jack?"

It wasn't a question I was prepared for. I barely knew the woman, though she'd told me enough of her recent history that I had a good idea of who she was. And while we had had a nice evening, I didn't want to give vibes that I was looking for something. I opened my mouth to decline, but the look on her face, hope, in its tiniest form, gave me pause.

"It might help us if you can drive?" Noelle said.

"Yeah, sure, I can drive you there."

Twenty minutes later, the desk sergeant at the police station had escorted us to a private waiting room. While in there, both women broke down. No matter how much you hated or felt apathetic toward someone you once cared bout, you had still once cared about them. Those feelings could slide back in without warning.

I had no idea what Noelle's feelings toward her brother were. Presumably, she knew the history Katrine had shared with me. I'd also assume she cared about her niece, Bernie, and couldn't stand to see her brother be a douche to the kid.

Katrine's feelings were no mystery to me, though. And in this moment, breaking down without regard to who might hear, I knew what she was going through. We don't have to love someone to grieve for them. In her case, it was easier to believe he'd run off, maybe with a woman neither she nor his mistress knew about.

The women sobered when the detective opened the door. They held each other tight in a hug, whispering words of condolence and encouragement. They had to get through the next fifteen minutes. The officer asked them to follow him.

The women weren't sure they'd be able to keep it together, so they asked me to accompany them.

"This is for family only," the detective said.

"He's our cousin, from the US," Noelle said. "He just stopped to visit for a few days on his way to Paris."

The detective didn't believe her, but there appeared to be some connection between the two of them. He rolled his eyes and shook his head and gestured for us all to follow him.

When we reached the interview room, I got my first solid look at the detective. Something about him was familiar, though I couldn't place him. I hadn't been in town that long, but there were many faces. Locals and tourists. They all blended together. For me to have this level of recall, it had to have been for more than a few seconds, though.

He started speaking in Dutch, but quickly changed speeds when Katrine replied in English for my benefit.

"Right, so, well, ladies…" He fumbled with the folders on his desk, opening an unrelated case file and re-stacking the papers it held. "I guess I should just get on with it."

"Please, Theo, if you could. This is already hard enough."

"I'm sorry, Noelle." The two of them shared an extended glance before he set aside all but one folder. "This is not going to be easy. The body was, well, hell, not discernible. They couldn't find, um, the head."

Katrine brought a hand to her face and shielded her eyes. I tried to comfort her, but there was little anyone could do at that moment.

"I was told there was identifying information with him?" Noelle leaned forward as though she could see past the top document in the folder. "Is that not the case?"

Theo lifted the folder and stood it on end so that the contents were hidden. He looked away for a few moments before sighing and setting it back down then removing the paper covering the photos.

"There was no passport or ID. We didn't find a wallet. But, as everyone in here is probably aware, any beginner pickpocket could have made off with those. Or perhaps a brave looter climbed into that burned out room. But they did find a cell phone that seemed to be hidden, from what they tell me. It traced back to Nev. Also, we have these." He pulled three photos and set them side-by-side on the table. They were shots of body parts taken close enough to minimize the appearance of the trauma to the body and instead focus on the tattoo, a symbol I couldn't discern that appeared to be inked on his calf.

Katrine wiped fresh tears from her eyes.

"Can you confirm that Nev had this tattoo?"

Katrine confirmed with a nod and said nothing.

Theo slid the photos together and closed them inside the folder, which he then placed inside his desk drawer. "Sorry to have done that, but we need to provide a positive identification to the authorities in Barcelona."

"What will happen to his remains?" Noelle asked. "Do we have to claim them?"

Theo waved his hand across the desk. "We'll take care of all that. He'll be transported home so you can lay him to rest."

"You can leave him there for all I care." Katrine pushed back in her chair. "Are we done here?"

CHAPTER 13

I DROVE THE WOMEN BACK TO KATRINE'S. HER SISTER-IN-LAW asked me to wait, said she didn't think she could handle the drive home, and asked if I could take her. The car was clean, the night was dark, and I was feeling a little amped up after being inside a police station, so I agreed, thinking it would be a short jaunt and then a slightly longer walk home.

Ten minutes later, I knew that wasn't the case. After twenty minutes, I questioned where Noelle was taking me.

Seemingly reading my mind, she said, "We're almost there."

"Was starting to think we were lost."

"How would that make sense? I don't know where I live?"

"Just a comment, lady."

She breathed heavily. "You should leave her alone, you know."

"Who?"

"Don't who me. Katrine. She's been through too much as it is, and now this, finding out her husband is dead. She doesn't need another heartbreak."

"I'm not trying—"

"Sure, sure. You're not trying. Give me a break. Whatever she told you, believe half of it, and realize there is a lot more she is not telling you about her, Nev, and their life together. Turn here."

"You wanna fill me in?" The steering wheel slid through my fingers as the wheels straightened out after turning the corner. She pointed at the next street, another left.

"That's it right there. And, no, I will not fill you in. That is not my place or my responsibility." She opened the door and dropped a foot to the ground. "It is, however, your responsibility to consider her in any actions you take. She's delicate. Remember that."

"Like I was trying to say, I'm—"

"There's a parking lot a half mile from Katrine's on the same road we took out. Leave the car there, keys in the glove box. I'll retrieve it later."

"Wait, what if—"

She slammed the door shut and disappeared into the darkness.

"The hell just happened?" I muttered.

The drive back to town felt quicker. That's how it always went. The unfamiliar and unusual causes time to slow down. It's the everyday stuff that makes it feel like our lives are passing faster than we can keep up with. How many memories does anyone have of driving to work? But wildflowers along the highway median while dad drives the cruiser across country during summer vacation?

Never forget them.

I half-expected to find a severed hand in the glove box when I opened it. No such luck, though. Just the owner's manual and a bag of cleaning wipes. I tucked the keys behind both and made my way back to Katrine's. It was a straight shot down the road, like Noelle had said. The air was crisp and fragranced with the damp smell of incoming rain. Thick clouds raced overhead. The full moon fought to shine through but remained a diffused light hovering over the area.

When I reached the outer edge of town, I pulled out my phone and sent a quick text to the number Clarissa had given to me.

Any updates? Things are getting weird here.

Time slowed again as I waited for a response. Over the recent months, Clarissa had made fewer appearances in my thoughts. I didn't necessarily want it that way. It just happened. It kept me saner. Sharper.

The same was true of her physically being around. It dulled my senses too much. We'd been through the relationship spectrum over the years. On and off again. Mostly my fault. Actually, all my fault. I came and went in her life, all the while certain she'd solve every problem I ever had. Temporarily. And when all of those problems came rushing back to find me unaware, there'd be another host of issues that had popped up to pile on. And that would lead the relationship to be doomed. That's why I never let it go that far. She meant too much to me to do that.

I'd almost given up on a quick reply when the phone buzzed in my hand.

We think something is happening and it might be centered in Bruges. Keep your head on a swivel. I'll be in touch soon.

That required no response from me, so I shoved the cell back in my pocket and stepped past the first pool of light spilling onto the old street leading to my rental. Not wanting to draw any more attention to myself, I wove around the lights and stuck to the shadows.

It was quiet. Peaceful. Empty. Most windows were dark. I imagined it might be different in summer, when tourists flocked to the town. But right now, this was perfect.

When I reached the rental, I stood outside for a few minutes, deciding whether to knock on Katrine's door and see if she needed company.

"Probably not the right move."

The fact I said it out loud meant it was true. She'd be feeling hurt. Probably vulnerable. The last thing she needed tonight was me. Best to leave it alone.

So I did.

I unlocked my door and stepped into the heat, sliding my coat off and draping it over the railing. The hum of the furnace vibrated through the walls. The vent above me rained warmth down over my head. The drastic shift in temperature made my skin ache as though it were being pricked by pins.

I started toward the kitchen in the dark. I'd figured out a safe path through the house already. There was an uncorked bottle of wine on the island, but at this point, I was ready for a beer. I pulled one from the fridge, popped the top, and took a long swig.

It was then I flipped the light on and nearly dropped the bottle when I saw the blonde from earlier perched on the couch, legs crossed, a phone in one hand, pistol in the other. Both aimed at me.

"Jack Noble, right?"

CHAPTER 14

THE WHOOSHING OF MY BLOOD DROWNED OUT ALL OTHER sounds. I couldn't taste the beer anymore. My mouth had gone dry. My chest felt tight. Fingers tingled. For a man who'd lived life knowing I was one wrong move from death every moment, I shouldn't have had this reaction.

I shouldn't have frozen.

Her face remained calm, albeit with a spreading grin. She said my name again, more like a question this time, and with some inflection. Previously she had been so monotone I had figured she was seconds away from shooting me and would take no pleasure in it, as though I were a wounded animal blocking her path so she'd put it out of its misery.

"Did someone send you here?" I asked. "Are you keeping tabs on me?"

She shrugged and gestured with the pistol. "Wouldn't exactly need this out to keep tabs on you, would I?"

"Maybe."

She lifted an eyebrow.

"Probably not." I set the beer on the counter and stepped around it.

"That's far enough," she said. "In fact, why don't you go back to where you were standing."

"You can't see me there."

"I can see you well enough."

"What if I've got a 9mm stashed under here?"

"Reach for it. See what happens." She tightened her grip and gave up any semblance of trigger discipline.

"All right, we can do this your way for now."

She seemed deflated that I'd given in so easily. Why give her the satisfaction, though? Would she do something here? Empty her magazine? Not a chance. For one, too much time had passed. If she were here to kill me, the job would be done. Beyond that, the walls were shared. There was another row of houses less than twenty feet behind us. Too much risk of taking out a civilian. And even in an old section of town, plenty of residents had upgraded to Wi-Fi-connected doorbells that recorded video or had set up full security systems around their front and back doors. She'd be on camera the moment she left here.

The woman remained seated and said nothing. Her pistol remained trained on me though. Was she holding me there? Waiting for someone to arrive? There was no way she could get me out of the place. The gun held no power over me now. She'd have to holster it in an attempt to physically restrain me.

"We waiting on the big guy and his little buddy?" I asked.

She didn't reply.

"Or you got someone else coming?"

Still no reply.

I picked up my bottle and took a few sips, then took a few steps back, set the bottle down and crossed my arms over my chest. "What was it you said to me outside? Why am I screwing with your—"

"Interfering with my investigation."

"Right, your investigation. You don't look like a cop. Wouldn't be waiting in here like that, pistol out, no badge, if you were. You're not a local here. Accent is all wrong."

"My accent is whatever I want it to be," she said in thick Russian.

I lifted the beer bottle. "Cheers, comrade."

"What does it matter where I am from? I asked you not to interfere."

I nodded a few times. "Yeah, you're gonna have to be a little clearer with me. See, I grew up in Florida, so didn't really have the best school system. And I've had, I don't know, a dozen concussions, at least."

"Are you always this obnoxiously calm when someone has the ability to end your life with a simple squeeze of a trigger?"

"You're not gonna shoot me."

"Not here."

"Not anywhere."

"Why's that?

"You could've taken me outside, in the dark. Another layer of complexity has been added. So unless you've poisoned every surface in this place—" I dragged my finger across the countertop and licked it, "—which I doubt, by the way, then you're bluffing. And by bluffing, you're wasting your time and mine."

She sighed and stood. "Are you always this aggravating?"

"A trait I was blessed with at birth." We stood there staring at each other for several seconds. "Who the hell are you? Who do you work for? What do you want? And how do you know my name?"

"I think in our present situation, it is not you who should be asking the questions."

"Well, you aren't doing a whole lotta talking, lady. Someone's gotta get this party started."

"In time."

She had me at gunpoint, guaranteeing I'd keep my distance. The doorway interfered with any plans to get me out. It offered a chokepoint where the distance between us would shrink. Due to the placement of the stairs, she couldn't maintain more than six feet of distance between us while keeping me in her line of sight. Once my foot hit pavement, sprinting to the nearest corner would take a few seconds. Would she risk opening fire in the dark at a moving target in a place where chances of striking a civilian target were great?

I decided to up the ante. With as fluid a movement as I could muster, I pulled my pistol.

"Now we both have guns aimed at us. How about you answer those questions?"

She seemed unfazed. If anything, a smile crept onto her face for a few seconds.

"Who are you? Who do you work for? What do you want with me?

And how do you know my name?"

She remained seated and stoic, her pistol held steady, finger threading the guard.

I moved around the island and into the living room. She could take a knee shot, hobble me. Then when her partner arrived, they could drag me out, throw me into a car and get me somewhere to treat the wound. They had to be based out of somewhere in this town.

"Answer me." I moved closer to the door. "Or I'll walk out of here and you will never see me again."

"Are you sure about that?" This time she spoke in a Cockney accent. If it were her real one, it gave her backstory away. She came from a working class section of London, likely on the East End. "I found you in Bruges of all places."

"What are you talking about? You came at me, telling me to stay out of your investigation. It's nothing but coincidence we're both here."

She shrugged. "Is it? And is that what I said?"

I tipped my head back and pinched the bridge of my nose. "What the hell weird alternate universe did I step into?"

"You're kind of a disappointment, Jack. The way my handler used to talk about you...well, I was expecting something much different."

I stopped dead, lowered the pistol. Somehow this woman had a connection to me. Hundreds of faces raced through my memory. "Handler? Who are—"

Before I could complete the sentence and the connection, I felt a prick in my neck, then the world faded with little rice-size lines of white zigzagging in my vision until everything was black.

CHAPTER 15

THESE WERE THE NIGHTS LORRAINE HATED. NOT THE COLD. Not the rain. Not even being exposed to those elements with no chance to seek shelter. *"Not until the job is done."* Dylan's words echoed in her mind with the sound of the rain splashing in the puddles around her.

It was the anticipation of completing the job.

Her merino base layer trapped her body heat and helped keep her warm. Every layer past that was waterproof. She knew from experience, though, they would only keep the wetness at bay for so long. When the downpour was this torrential, she could expect it to soak through at some point.

Not worth thinking about, she reminded herself. Her attention turned to the last few hours with Dylan before he dropped her at the train station. She had no idea today would be *one of those days*. In fact, it was him who was to leave this evening. Destination unknown. A call from his DSGE contact meant he had to go, as there was a pressing issue. What he hadn't told her before carrying her off to bed was she would have to go elsewhere.

He knew what he was doing. She certainly would not have slept with him if she knew a few hours later she'd be a couple of hundred kilometers north, laying in an open field in Denmark in the rain while the Arctic air whipped in from the nearby coast with nothing to buffet the winds.

Bastard.

She smiled, though, knowing he was no bastard. Not to her. He had changed her life, and therefore she owed him. She hadn't been sure how she'd ever repay him for what he had done for her. Not until he took her to a private shooting range. The surprise on his face when she knew not only how to operate a wide range of firearms but also how to operate them with deadly accuracy had been worth the trip.

What came after...not so much.

Movement in the distance brought her focus back to the moment. Someone crossed in front of the light that shone down over the building's entrance. They didn't stop, though. Nor did they enter the building. They kept moving. She traced their path as they walked through each illuminated section of the walkway until they faded into the night.

She steadied herself with a few rounds of box breathing, in for four, hold for four, out for four. Dylan had taught her this. Said he was trained to use it when he was in Special Forces. Lorraine found that it settled her in all areas of life. She figured that repeated use of the technique strengthened the focus muscle it was building so when she was in a position like this one now, it would do the job quickly.

And it had worked fast, like she had hoped.

But her inattention would have led to a missed opportunity, or, even worse, an errant shot, had that person been her mark.

She had to pay attention. Focus. Not let memories, or dreams, or even the lure of her cell phone—she only had a burner on her anyway—disrupt her again.

Between the hours of eight and eleven. That's what she had been told. Two hours and fifteen minutes had passed. The man who she only knew as Cupcake would appear soon. And when he did, well, she tried not to think about that part of the job. For someone who was prone to overthinking and overanalyzing, she found that when it came time to pull the trigger, it was as though another person took over her body from far away and controlled her movements. Awareness did not leave her. She knew what was happening. But the images never stuck. They never became memories.

For that, she expressed gratitude every day.

The door to the building opened, and Lorraine homed in on the figures who exited. They lingered there, and she soon realized why. They were taking advantage of a pause in the rain for a smoke break. She had a sudden urge for one and stifled the sensation as soon as it crept up. She butted her right eye to the rifle scope to take a closer look. Neither of the men were her mark. She shifted her head back to center and resumed her watch, focusing on the light and how their movements disrupted it. Before long, they crushed their cigarettes under foot and reentered the building.

She wondered what went on in there. Was it a business of some sort? Definitely not retail, but possibly some kind of warehouse. The men didn't dress like bankers, that was for sure. What if it was a more sinister place? A group of criminals. Hackers, maybe. She preferred that story over the one where honest, hardworking folks were inside.

Because one of them was her target.

She retrieved the burner again and pulled her hood completely over her so it concealed any light emanating from the phone. She navigated to the photos folder, found the man's picture. He was young. At least, his clean-shaven face and boyish features made him look so.

What had he done?

Before that thought could root, Lorraine kicked it out of her head. Building a backstory for a mark could lead to nothing good. It simply did not matter. They did something to deserve what they were getting. She was only a vessel to deliver the verdict.

Yet, she couldn't help but wonder. Why? Was there something about him? She zoomed in on his face. It felt familiar. Surely, it was no one she had ever met. Perhaps it was his wholesome look.

Before she knew it, Lorraine could not shut off the part of her brain that overanalyzed everything. She went through the toolbox of techniques Dylan had taught her, yet none were working.

She placed the phone back in her interior pocket and removed the hood.

"Shit," she muttered.

A new group of bodies occupied the space around the front door. Again, she sighted through the scope and went from man to man, four in total, until she reached the last.

Her mark stood there, cracking a smile at something someone had said, cigarette dangling between his fingers.

She breathed four beats, held four beats, exhaled four beats. Repeated the process. The cigarette was at least halfway finished. There was another minute and a half, at least, to prepare. She'd use all of it if she had to. For one, she liked to have as much time to steady her breathing and heartrate as possible. And two, the setup was far from ideal. There were three others there. Three potential witnesses. She wasn't so far off they would have zero chance of seeing her as she fled. Someone was bound to spot the muzzle flash, even if from their peripheral. The complications that could arise were numerous, and none of them would make for an easy night for Lorraine.

Someone go inside, walk away, something.

Her mark took another drag off his smoke. She held her breath and released it when he lowered his hand and kept the cigarette by his side instead of flicking it into a puddle as one of the other men had just done before retreating to the warmth and dryness of the building.

The three remaining men repositioned, and not in a beneficial way for the job at hand. Her target was now concealed by a much larger man. Lorraine had no qualms with taking the larger man out, but the first shot *had* to be at her target. Anything that alerted him to her presence reduced the odds of her getting a kill shot. And without a kill shot, she might as well not return home. Though Dylan had never said as much, she suspected that a failed job—not an incomplete one where the target just never showed—would result in her own termination.

From behind the big man, the mark flicked his cigarette away. The door opened.

"Shit! Shit! Shit!" she muttered, now out of options.

She breathed in, held her breath, felt her heart beat fully then come to rest. And at that moment, she squeezed the trigger. The big man dropped as though someone had pulled the sidewalk out from under him.

Her mark spun around. The door hit him. Knocked him a foot or two to his right. He froze, arms out, as he stared at the lifeless and practically headless body of his coworker.

Lorraine breathed in. Held it. Felt her heart beat fully then come to rest for the second time.

She squeezed the trigger.

She exhaled the word, "Sorry."

Her mark dropped where he stood.

There was one man left. Poor sap. He'd only come out for a break. Didn't even smoke while he was out there. But he had to go, too.

Lorraine completed the process once more. She didn't even watch the guy drop this time. She scooped up her rifle and peeled herself from the muck she had been lying in and pulled the mask over her face. Twenty seconds later, she was rifling through the dead mark's clothing until she found what she had been dispatched for. Another card containing a seed phrase.

CHAPTER 16

THE SUBTLE PAIN OF AWARENESS CREPT OVER ME. THE PITCH-black room allowed my other senses to take over. Cool air pricked my skin. A heavy chemical smell, something like Lysol on steroids, burned my nostrils. The acrid taste in my mouth due to parched dryness. And silence so overwhelming it felt as though I was in a vacuum.

My head hurt like I had a hangover, but I'd dealt with worse. I started a full body scan searching for injuries, starting with my toes and fingers. All twenty wiggled and worked. My arms and legs moved freely. I reached out, found a wall, used it to rise out of the chair. I worked my way around the room, estimated it to be roughly twelve-by-twelve with one point of egress. Locked, of course.

I was alive. I could move around the room freely. But I was being held hostage. Pretty much everything I had expected out of Bruges.

Why was I here, though?

I had no recollection of ever meeting the blonde woman before. If I had crossed paths with her at any point in the past two decades, I would've remembered her. There were burly three-hundred-pound men I'd thrown off rooftops that I could picture clear as day. I'd surely recall an attractive blonde who partook in spy craft.

So why was she there? What was it she had said? She was disappointed based on the description of me from her handler. She knew of me.

It was all too convenient for coincidence. I hadn't stepped on her investigation, no matter what she said during our initial meeting. My guard had been down in that dive bar. Or, rather, I had been too focused on the goons. I recalled people coming and going but couldn't remember if she had been one of them, or if she had been there the entire time. Up until however long ago it was I had been rendered unconscious, her story of my interference had been plausible. It was in the realm of possibility that she had been at the bar waiting on those guys to show up. I altered their plans, thus altering her plans.

But how did that explain my current predicament?

What if she was in Bruges because of me?

This was the wormhole I feared most. That meant Clarissa or Beck had involved this woman. To watch over me? Perhaps. There was a way to get an answer, though. I reached into my pocket for the cell phone Clarissa had provided. It wasn't there. Had it been last night? I struggled to recall what I had on me other than my pistol when I reentered the rental.

"Think logically, Jack," I told myself.

I couldn't see Clarissa selling me out like this. She and Beck had found me. They could've disposed of me at any point after that and before putting me in the car to Bruges. And while I didn't trust Beck, both he and Clarissa seemed excited to have me on board for the op when we discussed it in the Keys. That was before I knew we had to endure a slight delay, which they apparently knew about at that time. What would be the point in pulling me out of the retirement I'd longed for, only to put me out of my misery in Belgium? I couldn't make the jump that they'd lied to have me killed. They could have done that anywhere.

It made no sense. None at all.

There was another possibility I hadn't considered until now. The man who had my records destroyed. Clive Swift. Could he have alerted a small group to my presence? He had the connections with government agencies to make me a generic citizen. What else could he accomplish if he wanted to?

But again, why?

If anything, he'd have found a way to recruit me into his organization. I'd have considered it, too. He and his people did good work. I got along with his field agents and felt I'd fit in with their organization. Plus, there was still Sasha's death to avenge and the mystery of who was at the top that wanted me, Bear, and her dead. Clarissa, too. The whole ruse to get her out of Italy still plagued me, as I'd yet to understand what exactly had happened.

I shook the thoughts from my head. It only led to a road where I threw my hands up trying to figure the point of any of this. And I was close to deviating from the current path to get there. Because the answer I'd come up with was this: There is no damn point. My place was no longer *here* in this world. I needed to get back to Mia and resume my new life.

The sound of the door unlocking mercifully saved me from my spiral.

Light flooded through the opening door. Daggers penetrated my eyes as I adjusted. I blinked hard as the recesses of the room came into view. Fresh air rushed in, warm and fragrant. A man stepped in carrying a tray with food. Looked like a burger and some fries. My stomach groaned.

He set the food down and left, leaving the door open a crack. A test? An invitation? Doubtful. Someone else was coming.

I grabbed the burger, discarded the bun and ate the patty in a few bites without regard to whether it had been poisoned.

The blonde entered, her face a mix of surprise at the burger bun on the tray and disgust at my distended cheeks as I worked my way through the patty.

"Guess I don't need to ask if you were hungry." She spoke with the same London accent.

I forced the food down and cracked the top off the water bottle and chugged it all at once.

"Figure I should get it while I can. Not sure how hospitable you all are to your guests."

She smirked. "I like a man with a sense of humor."

"You'll love me then. That's the only sense I got."

She looked over her shoulder and nodded at whoever whispered to her. A moment later, a chair appeared. She wheeled it to the center of the room after closing the door and sat down.

"You're pretty calm considering you're alone with me," I said. "You know my name. Must know a bit about my background."

"In the time it would take you to reach me, they would be alerted." I followed her glance upward and spotted the security camera. "The room would flood with a non-lethal but powerful gas that would render both of us unconscious. I would be treated immediately. You would suffer side effects for a few days, and that would guarantee you never try something like that again."

I continued to scan the ceiling and walls, noticing an unusual number of vents, indicating she was not bluffing. The fact that the room was outfitted with some sort of incapacitating gas meant they used this house frequently. Maybe she was working a case here.

"Plus, that would really screw up my plans for you," she continued. "We have work to do and time is quite short, I'm afraid."

"*You* have work to do. I just need to ride out my time in this town."

She dropped the smile, and her face tightened. "You'll do what we ask of you, Jack."

"All right, I gotta ask." I wiped the corner of my mouth with the back of my hand. "How the hell do you know who I am? I have no recollection of you, which is surprising if we've met before. I wouldn't forget your face. And, see, the thing is, no one is supposed to know who I am anymore. Either someone sold me out, or you really did know me. Which is it?"

"Sold you out?" She leaned back in her chair and crossed her arms. "No one that I am aware of."

"So, you randomly know me and we randomly ran into each other here in Belgium?"

She shrugged and the smirk returned to her face. "I may have been alerted you would be here."

"Who?" I paused and watched for any tell she might present. There was none. "You're not gonna answer that. How about this one. What do you know about me?"

"Jack Noble, the All-American boy. All-American football player, too. Quarterback. Eschewed college to join the Marines. Didn't last long in bootcamp, but not because you couldn't hack it. They saw something special in you. And Riley Logan."

She knew of Bear.

"You two were selected for a special program and shipped off to

Nowhere, West Virginia, where you were trained to operate in the shadows by the CIA in a now defunct highly controversial program intended to allow them to circumvent certain rules which prevented them from performing certain operations in the United States. In time, your mission shifted from being in the lead to doing whatever your team leader assigned to you. You were sent overseas in a diminished role. After incidents there and on home soil, you left the program and joined Frank Skinner in the SIS."

She knew of Frank.

"That lasted for a few years until the time Riley left the CIA program. After that, you two sometimes worked together, at first contracting with Frank and other agencies. But in time, it became a free-for-all. You lost your morals and served the highest bidder. That worked out as you'd expect, and in time, you found your way. I suppose you found your redemption when you assassinated Skinner in broad daylight."

She knew of my final confrontation with Frank.

"Then you disappeared and completely fell off the radar. I thought maybe you were dead. Lord knows you've outlasted all your available lives, so it wasn't a surprise. But then I realized you weren't dead, and you weren't a ghost. You just simply never were."

She knew my records were wiped.

"So, I paid extra attention. I figured you couldn't handle life away from all this for too long. You'd resurface. And you did. One small piece of intel, and I had your location."

Her last sentence implied she was here because of me. That made no sense when considering the room we were in. Perhaps I was here because of her?

"You've done your research." I drummed a fry on the tray. "But how did you—"

"I didn't have to do research. I've witnessed a lot of this. I watched from the stands, but I watched, nonetheless."

Frustration was boiling over. "How? Who are you?"

"We have met before, Jack. You don't remember, which means I had learnt well and did my job properly."

"When? Where?"

"While you were a member of the SIS, and for a time after, you worked with my mentor often."

The timeframe. Her accent and nationality. There was one possibility.

"Dottie?"

She nodded.

"So, you're MI5? MI6?"

She shook her head. "Not anymore."

"Then who do you work for?"

"Who says I work for anyone?"

"All right, look, I'm dealing with, at minimum, a drug induced hang-over here. I need you to spell this out for me. Are you here because of me?"

"Yes, but not for the reason you think."

CHAPTER 17

"A NUMBER OF YEARS AGO, YOU APPREHENDED A ROGUE FBI agent who was working with a terrorist cell in the United States and abroad. Do you remember?"

"Joe Dunne." Images of being waterboarded sprung to mind first. And then Reese McSweeney, who'd I'd seen not too long ago in Texas—just before the Frank Skinner incident—when the Jeep I'd been driving across the country died. It set into action the events which led to me being here now, instead of with McSweeney, who I'd likely never see again, as the FBI showed up and whisked her away to another location under a new identity. I pushed the thoughts aside. "I don't know if I'd use the word apprehended."

"Doesn't matter," she said. "What does is that there was fallout from the incident."

"You're not lying."

"Pardon?"

I waved her off. "Never mind. What's this about fallout?"

"A Dutch man by the name of Dylan Van de Berg was a close associate of Dunne and the terrorists in Paris."

"What kind of associate?"

"A contract associate."

"An assassin."

"Correct. He may have even had you in his sights at one time."

I shrugged. "So, a shitty assassin."

"I wouldn't go that far. He does his job very well. Even when we can prove he's involved, there is no trail to follow in or out. Meaning, we typically don't know how he's getting the jobs and who he's getting them from."

"How do you know that it's him?"

"His bullets are unique. Every single one has the same markings." She produced her phone and pulled up a video. "This was filmed last night from a security camera."

The scene that played out showed a group of men standing in the cold, smoking a cigarette in front of a warehouse. After one left, the other three were killed in rapid succession. Someone approached in few seconds after and seemed to take something from one of the bodies.

"What do you take from that?" she asked.

"The guy by the door was the target. Had to dispose of the big man to get him. They hit him with a shot guaranteed to shock the others. Most people aren't used to seeing a human head explode in front of them."

She agreed with my assessment.

"What is this place?" I asked. "Looks like a run-of-the-mill warehouse."

"They're cutting common street drugs and illegal prescription drugs with Fentanyl in there. But we think that's scratching the surface. Behind this, there appears to be a massive laundering operation going on."

"So, your guy's doing the world a favor, then."

"Be that as it may, his intentions are hardly noble ones. It's all about money. Whether he was paid by a rival group of dealers, or the government, he did the job for the money."

"What's this have to do with Bruges? With Tweedle Dee and Tweedle Dumb, who I keep running into?" I ran my hand through my hair and grabbed the back of my neck. "What's it got to do with me?"

"With you, not so much, I think. With Bruges, it is believed that Van de Berg has frequented the town often in recent years. Perhaps he has a hideout here. It's a small town in the grand scheme of things. It enjoys travelers who both stay for days at a time, as well as cruise ship day-trippers. He could be anonymous here from those possibly hunting him."

"When's the last time you or anyone had a visual on Van de Berg?"

She looked down and shook her head. "It's been years. Some theorize he had his appearance altered and that he regularly wears disguises."

"Theories," I said. "No one knows for sure."

"Correct."

I leaned back and rubbed my eyes. "This is fascinating, but I don't understand why you had to knock me over the head and detain me in order to tell me this."

"You nearly crossed paths with Van de Berg years ago, best we can tell. He was there in Luxembourg City to kill you. I need to know whether you actually had personal interaction with him prior to that. If so, you might be able to help us take him down."

I pushed my chair back and stood. Before I was all the way up, the door opened. She waved the man off. "Let me get this straight. You assault me, and now you're asking me for help?"

"I didn't want it to go down like this, Jack. I was prepared to tell you all of this last night. You're the one who pulled a gun on me. Didn't leave us much choice, did you?"

"While you were holding me at gunpoint." I paused for a moment. "You don't see the irony there?" I sat back down. "Anyway, what about the two goons going around town harassing people? They're putting people out of business. What do they have to do with any of this?"

"I think something."

"You *think*? What is this? Amateur hour? And you seriously worked for Dottie?"

Her cheeks reddened. Now that I knew her mentor, I could get under her skin at will.

"We have to start somewhere, Jack. They're obviously working for someone, and I think it is somehow all connected."

"You may be right." I now knew I was dropped in Bruges for a reason, and they hadn't received new intel as Clarissa alluded to in our last text exchange. And that reason was not to hide out and lay low while Clarissa and Beck until they got the op back on track. There was something here. What if I didn't find it? What would happen?

"Will you work with us, Jack?" She assumed a relaxed posture, but the anticipation cracked through her voice.

"Who the hell are you? I don't even know your name."

"Elizabeth Yates."

"Who do you work for, Mrs. Yates? Still with MI6?"

"Miss. And I'm an independent contractor these days, though I have several contacts in the agency still."

"You're working for some group, right?"

"Not at all."

"Then who sent you here?"

"Myself." Her eyes narrowed. Her face steeled. Her cheeks were red again, but with anger. "This is personal. One of those bullets killed my last partner in MI6."

I studied her for a minute to determine whether it was all an act. "If I help you—and that's a big if at this point—but if I do, what's in it for me? What happens after?"

"The joy that comes with knowing you helped a lass in need?" She gave a brief smile before turning serious again. "You don't have to do this if you don't want. But know that I don't believe in coincidences. You are here for a reason whether you know it or not. Maybe you were even set up." She held up a hand stopping my protest before I could start. "Don't say she'd never do something like that to you. You don't know what forces Clarissa is dealing with."

My mind reeled. How had this woman gone from not quite sure who I was, to knowing not only exactly who I was, but also that Clarissa had sent me?

"Look, I'm not saying that I do," she continued. "But perhaps you need a reminder that the people in charge rarely give two shits about any of us. No matter how well you do your job, you are disposable. I think we've both learnt that."

Perhaps her independent status had been forced.

The lengths she had gone to in order to secure this sit-down with me were extreme. Yet, I didn't get the feeling someone would come in and place a bullet between my eyes if I declined her offer.

"Can I get some time to think it over?"

She exhaled, and her chin dropped to her chest. She muttered something before saying, "I'll go make some coffee. Will that help?"

"You've been stalking me for a while, haven't you?"

She rolled her eyes. "You don't remember me at all, do you?"

"I was busy back then. Distracted."

"I brought you guys coffee a few times when you were in London with Dottie." She pulled her hair back tight. "Picture my hair black and way too much makeup on my face."

"Shit, maybe I do remember you."

"I'll be back in five. Hopefully you'll have made up your mind?"

"No need. I'm in. Where do we start?"

CHAPTER 18

THE MORNING SUN TRIGGERED A FLASH OF PAIN THROUGH MY eyes and head as I stepped out of Elizabeth's place with a full thermos of coffee in hand. They had offered to drive me. I declined. She provided directions that were simple enough to follow in my current state. We'd meet up later in the day to begin operations.

A chill remained in the air but was rapidly burning off. There were several people already out, phones and cameras in hand, taking pictures of the buildings leading to the square, the place where tourists flocked and the worst food in Bruges could be had.

I presumed, at least.

Thankfully, my route carried me away from all of that.

Twenty minutes later, I arrived at the rental. The door had remained unlocked all night. Didn't matter. Anything a thief could find, they could have. They wouldn't be able to locate the essentials, which were either on me or hidden. I did a once-over of the place, dumped the rest of the coffee, then showered and changed. After that, I stepped outside into the garden. The plan had been to knock on Katrine's back door. But she was already outside.

She sat on a chair, reclined back, reading a book. The title was in Dutch or German. I couldn't figure it out. She closed it over her thumb and tried to smile at me while shielding her eyes from the light.

"How're you feeling?" I asked, not sure what else to say.

"I'm still processing. That wasn't news I expected to receive."

"Who would?"

"There were times that I...I had hoped Nev was dead. Of course, I'd say this and feel guilty and beg God forgiveness for being such an awful woman."

I dragged a chair across the patio and sat across from her. "Everyone thinks like that. Hardly anyone will admit it."

"I'm special, I guess?"

"Fair assessment."

"Coffee?"

I feigned a yawn and didn't bother telling her I'd already downed a pot. More wouldn't hurt. "Yeah, I could use some."

"One moment." She stood and entered her house.

I took a peek to see if anyone else was inside. It appeared empty.

Katrine returned with a carafe and two European-sized coffee mugs. She smiled, holding the carafe up. "You seem to drink a lot of coffee, so figured this would be good."

"I was born with a cuppa joe in hand." I took the carafe and filled both mugs. "Mom said she couldn't keep me away from the stuff."

Katrine laughed. "Really?"

"Part of growing up an Army brat, I suppose. Gotta be able to handle your caffeine"

"Were you in the military?"

I nodded as scenes of my career flashed in my mind. "Did some time in the Marines, followed it up with government work."

"And now? What is it you do?"

"Not much at all anymore."

"I thought running a business would keep a person busy? I know it did me."

I'd become too relaxed around her. "Get the right people in the right positions, and it's gravy. Never been more relaxed than I am now." I didn't bother to tell her the effects of last night's blow to my head were contributing to that. What I needed was rest. But that could wait.

She plopped back in her seat with a heavy sigh. The legs grated on the stone floor. "You ever wonder how we got here?"

"Well, you came through that door—" I hooked my thumb over my shoulder, "—and I came through that one."

Katrine shook her head. "Are you always this corny?"

"Only on Tuesdays."

"It's Thursday."

"Damn." I glanced down at an imaginary watch. "Gotta get this thing fixed."

A smile lingered on her face for a few seconds too long. It faded as she pulled the mug to her lips and inhaled the steam. Her eyes fluttered before her gaze settled back on me. "I appreciate what you are doing. Easing my mind, and all that. I need the distraction."

"Why don't you get changed, and you and I can head out for a late breakfast?"

Thirty minutes later, we were a mile away, walking in silence through the busying streets. The morning chill had burned off. It was quite mild outside of the shadows.

Katrine was first to speak. "That's one of my favorite places, right there." She aimed her finger down the street.

"The bagel place?"

"No, just past that. Owned and operated by my grandmother's best friend for practically her whole life. She doesn't do much of the work anymore, but she's there. Every single day, that woman is there. Some people have been eating in that little bistro for fifty years. Can you imagine?"

"Hard to imagine anything on that long of a timeline."

Her brow furrowed. "What an odd thing to say."

"Is it?"

The reality of her world and the news she received the night before struck her. I could see the color drain from her face, leaving it a few shades lighter. "I suppose not."

"Sorry. I should've known that would hit the wrong way after last night."

"No, it's OK. Come on." She grabbed my hand and picked up her pace.

Before long, we pushed through the front door, a set of bells jingled and announced our presence.

There were seven tables packed into the dining area. Six were full. Katrine pointed to the empty one, which was farthest back, and asked me to claim it. Getting to it took more effort than I cared to expend. There weren't any other choices, though. The woman was set on eating here, so I did as she asked.

She came to the table with another mug of coffee for me and a plate of bacon. Might've been the best I'd ever had. Not sure what they coated it with, brown sugar, maybe. I savored each and every piece.

Katrine started waving someone over. The old woman stepped out from behind the counter, making sure her hair was perfect as she wove through the dining room. She was maybe ninety pounds and barely five feet tall and she still moved like a young dancer. Her smile was bright, even if her eyes weren't anymore. She greeted me and pointed up at a photo behind my head. I twisted in my seat to see the image of a beautiful woman, mid-thirties, standing in front of the building. It was her, and it had been taken the day she opened the bistro.

As we were talking about the old days, her friendship with Katrine's grandmother, and her secret bacon recipe, the atmosphere in the place changed. A few tables got up and left, leaving plates full of food behind. Katrine reached for my hand mid-sentence and grabbed my attention.

"It's them," I said, cutting off the old woman.

Past her, my two new buddies stood out front. The shorter one used the window as a mirror while he picked his teeth. The big guy glanced around the room until he spotted me. A grin spread across his wide face.

"Not those sons of bitches," the old woman said. "So tired of them. How many times must I tell them no?" She shook her fist in the air.

"This will be the last." I got up, walked around the tables, toward the door.

What happened next, I never could've imagined.

CHAPTER 19

THE BIG GUY SNARLED AT ME AS HIS HAND HIT THE DOOR. HIS partner was off to the side, adjusting the pistol in his waistband. Was that necessary for the old lady?

No.

For me?

Yeah.

But it didn't come to that.

Both men flinched. Not sure how I even saw the movement. Because the next thing that happened was the big guy's face smashed into the door and his body went limp. His partner pulled his pistol and spun, but it was too late. He dropped to the sidewalk. A red stain bloomed on his shirt. Blood trickled from a hole in his head. By this point, the big guy had rolled to the side, slid off the door, and hit the ground. He came to rest near his partner.

The bistro's remaining patrons were gasping or crying or screaming in terror. I heard my name being called repeatedly. Sounded as though it came from a block away.

"Get down," I yelled as I backed away from the door and drew my gun. "Everyone, knock your table over and get behind it."

The sound of the metal trim that surrounded the French bistro tables clanking on the floor replaced all human emotion. For the moment, these people had a purpose to occupy their frightened brains.

I stepped behind the counter. There were windows, but at least I had some additional cover from the stainless-steel racks that lined the outer edge of the kitchen and prep area. The racks were filled with pots, pans, boxes of flour, and onions. From a safe vantage point, I scanned the street as far as I could in both directions. It was a ghost town. The shooter had either fled, or they had shot from inside a building or a roof across the street.

Logic said the shooter had fled. Two shots had been fired and several seconds had passed. Every moment mattered when making an escape. By now, they could be a block away. The radius would grow, making it less likely they were apprehended.

But reason and logic left men dead when they'd return home otherwise had they listened to their gut.

"Do you think he's gone?" Katrine called out.

"Doubt it," I said. "If you have room behind you, scoot your table back. I want everyone as far away from the front glass as you can get."

"Why?" someone called out.

I barely heard them over the screaming in my head that told me to get down now. I turned and retreated farther into the kitchen, diving to get out of view of the window. A second later, the glass exploded and rained down over my legs. It sounded like a Texas hailstorm in July. I looked for the entry point and found it when I saw flour pouring from a bag I was staring at moments ago.

Screams and cries erupted from the dining room again. They intensified when another round penetrated the glass in front of them. I heard two more rounds collide with the floor, saw the dust and debris kicked up three feet from the door. This indicated the shooter was on the roof and he was aiming down. He had limited sight into the restaurant.

If the two goons were the only targets, the shooter would've fled already. But they took a shot at my position, then again into the main dining room, presumably in an attempt to draw me out.

I couldn't be sure I was the target. They might've been shooting at anything that moved. Unless they were aware of who I was. In which case, they'd assume the only one moving anywhere toward them was me.

Unless Elizabeth was behind this—which didn't make sense; she could've killed me earlier—someone else knew my location and had managed to tail me to the restaurant. Were they specifically waiting for the two men to arrive? Did they send the two men to the restaurant and then kill them? Or were the goons a bonus kill?

It wasn't often the commotion of sirens comforted me, but I felt relieved at the first faint sound of them. My muscles unclenched enough that I drew in a deep breath. The police closed the distance quickly. The wailing echoed off the buildings and inside the room until it had reached a fever pitch that threatened to rupture my eardrums. Based on sound, I'd say there were at least ten units pulling up. An ambulance, too. One by one, the sirens cut off. Doors slammed. A senior officer barked orders.

The shooter had taken off by now. No doubt about that.

After the first few uniforms entered, Katrine came running to me. She threw herself into my chest, wrapped her arms around my neck, and proceeded to lose her balance and footing thanks to the mess on the kitchen floor.

"All right," I whispered, smoothing down her hair. "It's all right now. The cops are here."

She pulled back until our faces were a few inches apart. There were tears in her eyes. "Those men, they were the ones who—"

"I know. They used to harass you. Other businesses, too. Guess this place was on their route."

Katrine whipped her head side to side.

"What?" I asked.

"They never messed with this place."

"Maybe that's why they got shot then."

"No. Believe me, Jack. No."

"Hang on a sec." My phone had been buzzing in my pocket since the first shot. I had a few missed texts from Elizabeth.

Jack, it's E. Where are u?

Let me know you're safe. There's been a breach. Shooter at large.

We have to get out of here. Now. I'll track you on your phone.

I found your location. Go out the back door. I'll be there.

Muscles clenched again. Breathing became restricted. My heart rate increased. How could she know where I was? How could she get here so quickly?

"What is it?" Katrine asked.

"You're not safe."

I regretted saying the words the moment they came out of my mouth. It was a huge assumption. One that could pose a massive risk if Katrine believed me. And maybe worse if she didn't. Odds were, those men were here to take my life, and that had nothing to do with Katrine. But we'd spent time together outside of her house. We were at the police station together last night. We walked through town together today.

A chill ran down my spine as though a trickle of glacier water had found its way inside my shirt. What if this had something to do with her husband's death? What if it were no mistake he was in that building the moment the bomb went off?

"Jack?" She gripped my arm and shook it. "What do you mean?"

"You're gonna have to trust me, Katrine. I don't think your husband was in the wrong place at the wrong time. And I don't think that's the case right now with you, either."

Most of the police presence was focused on the two bodies on the sidewalk. One was inside taking statements. They had the exit blocked.

"How well do you know the restaurant?"

She was looking all around, fear and panic in her eyes and on her face. "What?"

"How can we get out of here without the cops seeing us?"

"The cops? What?"

She was slipping further into shock. I had to pull her back to reality.

"Is there an office?"

Her head twitched a couple of times, then her eyes locked on mine. Her hand slid down to my wrist. She grabbed my hand and pulled me further through the kitchen. We turned a corner and she yanked a door open. The narrow space had a small desk with a computer on it and several yellowing notebooks in three separate piles. A few were knocked to the ground as we hurried toward the door at the far end.

"Through here." She turned the knob and threw her hip into the metal frame. It banged open and slammed against the building.

I followed Katrine out, spotted the van as it drove past a large dumpster. The glare on the windshield concealed the occupants. I threaded my finger through the trigger guard.

If anyone but Elizabeth greeted us when that van came to a stop, they were dead.

CHAPTER 20

DYLAN HAD BROKEN DOWN THE RIFLE AT THE FIRST SOUND OF sirens and now had discarded most of it in back-alley dumpsters each a half-mile apart as he fled through the maze that was his escape route. Along the way, he retrieved the bag containing a change of clothes and backup credentials. He rarely needed them, but one could not be too careful.

After Lorraine's success the previous night, not only taking out her target but also another high-level member of the organization and disguised her true efforts there, he decided to press his luck in Bruges. He tipped off the henchmen, Luis and his partner, to Noble's whereabouts. Told them he'd pay them the hundred thousand they requested to complete the job. They were a part of the same crime group, pushing that lethal fentanyl concoction from Brussels to Bruges. Killing them here benefited Dylan in two ways. Luis was one of the only people who knew specifically that Noble was here and Dylan was going to kill him. Also, it would take some of the heat off the warehouse investigation. It might look like an inside job, that someone within the organization was cleaning up loose ends. Plus, his cousin, who he learned had been identified as one of the victims in the bombing, might have tipped them off to the job in Barcelona, saying he'd be able to repay them soon. In his gut, he felt Noble was here because of that.

He also killed them for pleasure. And a little good karma. After everything else he'd done in his life, he could use it. Not that he believed in it.

He messed up, though. He should've gotten Luis and his partner after they took out Noble. So as it was, he'd missed Noble. Again. The first time had been in Luxembourg not too many months back. Schreiber, the reporter, took that bullet. Noble managed to escape the city and unwound what had been months of planning on a contract that had been active since the day Noble had killed Frank Skinner.

It still was, despite the directive to destroy Noble's files and offer him some sort of immune status. There were certain groups that did not recognize such efforts, and the contract maker fell into that category.

It had remained in effect, and once again, Dylan blew his chance.

He did not look forward to explaining how Noble got away. And as much as he enjoyed killing the other two men, it might make the situation worse. People, even those who were willing to pay for another man to die, did not appreciate collateral damage. Chances were, this would not please the maker. Especially not with the mark narrowly avoiding his demise once again.

Dylan would handle it. He always did. His track record spoke for itself. He'd be given another chance.

He reached the outskirts of town, now riding a skateboard while wearing baggy pants, an oversized hoodie, and a beanie that had actual human hair sewn in, giving him the appearance of a long-haired, past-his-prime burnout who skateboarded everywhere because he couldn't afford any other form of transportation.

Navigating down a quiet street, he slowed to a stop and retrieved his phone. There were a few missed calls. One from the contract maker. He'd deal with him later. More concerning were the five missed calls from Lorraine. He opened his messaging app to see if she'd tried there.

She hadn't.

Atypical, to say the least.

He got off the road and went about thirty meters deep into the woods and returned her call.

Upon answering in a breathless voice, Lorraine said, "Have you seen the news?"

"I was going to ask the same thing."

"Hold on." Her fingers danced across her keyboard. He pictured her opening the full round of news and social media sites. "I see you accomplished something. Terrorist attack seems to be the buzzword."

"Isn't it always?"

"There's even a witness claiming to see someone in a hijab. Were you wearing one as a disguise?"

He chuckled. "Of course not, but I like the direction the press is going with this. Let's see if we can slip in some misinformation to send them further down that rabbit hole."

The phone grated as she shifted it. When she returned, he could tell she had placed him on speaker. "Did you get—"

"Wait," he interrupted. "Before you speak, have you swept the apartment?"

"Yes, several times already." Contempt laced her voice, as it did every time he asked her if she had done something. She had told him it was condescending. Fine by him. He'd condescendingly ask every time if it meant they stayed free and alive. "There's nothing in here."

"I would still feel better if you took me off speaker."

"Hold on." She made the adjustment and most of the atmospheric noise faded. "Better?"

"Yes. I didn't get him, and I'm going to assume he'll put it together that he was the target. He'll be in the wind again."

"You found him quickly this time. That's a good thing."

"But my method of tracking him will soon disappear."

"Why?"

He hadn't filled Lorraine in on the details, because he never did. Once he had trained her, he left her to plan her own operations, as he did for his. Should one of them ever become compromised and break down under *questioning*, the other would not suffer as a result.

"Noble's good," he said. "Maybe one of the best. Once he's to a place he feels safe, he'll reevaluate every single step and find where he went wrong."

"I see," she said. "Is there anything I should do in preparation to help?"

He rubbed the stubble on his face as he considered this. Twice now, he'd had Noble in his sights and failed. But there were strict policies he had to adhere to. Policies he had created himself to provide separation from the job as well as the responsibility for taking lives.

But what were rules if not meant to be broken?

"I'm going to text a passcode," he said. "You know where to use it. You'll find information there. I want you to use it to isolate any patterns."

She agreed then sighed a few times. He knew this meant she had bad news for him. But what? Last night's operation had gone off perfectly, and she was already home in Amsterdam.

"What's wrong?" he asked.

"Your cover up in Barcelona," she said.

"What about it?"

"Did you know he had a tattoo?"

His stomach knotted. "Go on."

"His calf. Some stupid symbol."

"They've identified him, then? Even with the false identification I left on him?"

"Yes. And there was no ID found."

"Bastard doesn't deserve the recognition." He checked the time, knowing his ride would arrive soon. "If there is fall out from that—and I do anticipate there will be—I will deal with it. Finishing Noble once and for all is the top and only priority at the moment."

"But what about—"

"I said I'll deal with it. Forget about Nev and start tracking Noble as far as the signal will take us. I don't think it'll last long. Divert all resources into determining his next move." The sound of a car engine revving then settling into idle was nearby. "I've got to go."

"I love you," she said.

"Update me in an hour."

CHAPTER 21

THE VAN'S SIDE DOOR SLID OPEN. ELIZABETH POKED HER HEAD out and waved us forward. I moved, but Katrine held fast with her hand wrapped around mine. I looked back at her. Her face was a mix of shock and fear and panic.

"We have to go" I said. "Gotta trust me, Katrine."

"Jack, what's happening?" Tears streamed down her cheeks. "Why were those men killed like that? Why did they keep shooting? Are you a target?" She waited for a response I didn't give her. "Who are you?"

"Look, I'll tell you everything, but we have to get in that van now."

She released my hand and stumbled backward, letting out a howl when she tripped and hit the wall.

"Come on, Jack," Elizabeth said. "They'll block the roads soon. Just leave her."

"One minute," I yelled over my shoulder. Then I turned back to Katrine. "I don't think you're safe here, and it's not because of me. Something was set in motion. Maybe when your husband left. Possibly even before that. But it's no mistake or coincidence you got word last night his body had been found, and today, someone is trying to kill us."

With wide eyes, she glanced around as though the answer could be found in the air in front of her. "Us?"

"Whoever it was, they got away. They're nowhere near here now. But

I'm guessing if they were ballsy enough to pull this attempt mid-day, they'll be back. Soon." I extended my hand. "Come on. At least let us get you away from here. We can drop you at your sister-in-law's or someplace else safe."

Seconds felt like minutes in a never-ending day. Another round of sirens rose in from the distance. They were shutting down the roads. I didn't have the area memorized completely, but I knew this alleyway had multiple egress points that would be cut off sooner rather than later. We had to go. I didn't want to leave Katrine behind. Not after what had happened in the past twelve hours or so. Not with a killer on the loose. They'd fled by this point. No doubt. But to where, I had no clue. Could be down the street for all I knew.

"Katrine." I took a step back, arm still outstretched. "We gotta move now."

She nodded vigorously as her face steeled and her gaze settled on me. She reached for my hand, and I pulled her forward, shifted, propelled her into the van. Elizabeth caught her and helped her to the rear row of seats. I climbed in after, started toward the back. Elizabeth put her hand on my shoulder.

"Sit up here," she said when I craned my head around to look at her. "We need to discuss next steps."

"I'm sure part of that is getting whatever intel you can out of me."

She said nothing.

"There isn't much, lady. But we'll talk." I leaned close to her ear. "Let me get her settled, make sure she's OK. I'll get her to turn her phone off."

"Good thinking." Elizabeth slammed the door shut and settled into the seat diagonally behind the driver. "Escape route B," she said to him. "Let's get outside of town limits ASAP."

He nodded, dropped the shifter into drive and peeled away. A bit risky, maybe. But the cops were otherwise occupied and not likely to pay attention to the sound of tires spinning.

I dropped in next to Katrine and helped her with the seatbelt buckle.

"Thank you," she whispered.

"Doubt you mean that." I met her eyes, smiled. She tried to return it, but her lips barely moved. "I know this must seem crazy."

She nodded. "What is happening?"

"I'm not sure."

"Who are you? Is this because of you?"

"It might be." I searched for the right words, a way to explain to her who Jack Noble really was. "My story is complicated, Katrine. I'm not a business owner. Not in the typical sense, at least. When I was fresh out of high school, I enlisted in the Marines. Things were rough going in Recruit Training, and me and another guy were pulled out and sent to a secret Agency training facility."

"Agency? The CIA?"

"Yeah. It was a job. I was in it until I wasn't. Made a few friends and plenty of enemies along the way. Things went sideways and I had to go into hiding. Eventually, I reached out to a reporter to tell my side of the story. We agree to meet in Luxembourg City. A bullet meant for me hit him."

Her eyebrows rose as she gasped. "I remember this. It wasn't that long ago."

I glossed over the rest as I caught us up to the present. "I didn't choose your place. Someone else did. And the fact you've told me it hadn't been rented in a while makes me think someone was interfering, holding it, until I they could put me here."

"Who? How?"

"I don't know the answer to those questions, but they scare the shit out of me, Katrine."

"Why?"

"Because of the last people I had contact with. The ones who brought me here."

"Do you trust them?"

"One of them. Trust her with my life."

"The others?"

"I'm nothing but a pawn to them. A means to an end. They want me around long enough for them to get what they want. After that, I'm probably as good as dead."

"Why did you agree to come with them? Did they leave you no choice?"

"Not directly, no."

"What's that mean?"

I thought of how to phrase it. After all, I was supposed to be off the grid. No records. No one tracking my movements anymore. "I was offered a chance at a new life. A real life. Just me and my daughter. We were on our way to coasting for a few years when these people turned up in the Keys, telling me they needed my help. How my newfound status as an everyday guy would allow me to use my skills to accomplish a major goal."

"You couldn't resist?"

"I wanted to. Believe me, I did." I thought of Mia's face. Her smile. How every day I was missing her growing up. How soon she wouldn't want me around. "If they found me, others could as well. See, I was using them as much as they were using me. By providing aide to their operation, they'd be bound to assist me with cutting the head off of whatever organization still wanted me dead. It wasn't enough to have the anonymity of a clean file. I've gotta eliminate any remaining threats to my existence."

Katrine leaned her head back against the side of the van. She blinked her way through processing everything I had said. "Jack, this is so heavy."

I laughed. "You ain't lying, sister."

"So, these people—" she pointed to the front of the van, "—these are people you've known before?"

I shook my head. "A run-in or two in the past, but nothing more."

Her forehead wrinkled. "You trust them?"

"We're here, aren't we?"

"I hope you're right, Jack." She looked down at the empty seat between us. "I've got Bernie to think of, and…"

"Hey, don't worry. I'm gonna talk with Elizabeth in a few minutes and get all of this straightened out. We'll get you somewhere safe. We'll arrange for security for your mother-in-law and daughter." I bit the inside of my cheek while searching for the words for my next request. "But we can use your help, too."

"Me? What can I do?"

"I don't know how your husband is tied to this, but somehow he is. It's not a coincidence his body was identified after I arrived. It's not a coincidence that the goons who used to harass you guys were taken out in front of us. And they might not have even been the targets."

She leaned in closer. Whispered. "How do you know she's not involved with them?"

"I know who she used to work for." Though, given how things turned out with Dottie in the end, their relationship didn't give me the comfort I searched for. "I believe she's here for the right reasons, even if I'm unclear about them. We're all on the same side, though. I'll help them. They'll help me. We'll all help you. And I need you to do me a favor, for all of our safety. Power down your phone."

She nodded as she adjusted herself in the seat to retrieve her phone. "OK, Jack. Keep me safe. That's all I ask."

From the front of the van, Elizabeth said, "Jack, it's time. We need to discuss a new development."

CHAPTER 22

ALL SIGNS POINTED TO AMSTERDAM, A TWO-AND-A-HALF-HOUR drive, according to Elizabeth. For a while, they had been tracking a pair of cell phones. A call had been intercepted shortly after the shooting, revealing the city as the next destination. Unfortunately, the cell phone used in Bruges had remained behind. Didn't matter. They had narrowed down an address. A hotel somewhere in the northern section of the city.

Amsterdam was a place I wasn't too familiar with. If all went well, that wouldn't pose a problem. We'd uncover a treasure trove of information and put this investigation to bed.

I had nodded off at some point. The deceleration and bouncing of the van as we exited the motorway jostled me awake. Elizabeth sat next to me. When she noticed me stirring, she reached into her pocket and pulled out a mint tin.

"Have one," she said.

"The hell are these?" I slid the lid open and was greeted with menthol.

"Mints."

"You saying my morning breath is that bad?"

She laughed. "Yes, but that's beside the point. These'll speed up the waking process."

"Or leave me dead."

"If I wanted you dead—"

"Yeah, yeah. You'd have done it hours ago." I popped a mint into my mouth and hoped for the best.

"It's a close second to coffee."

"Nothing, my dearest Elizabeth, is a close second to coffee. There's coffee up here." I held my hand against the ceiling and then swooshed it down to the floor. "And every other stimulant here."

Her smile faded over the course of a few seconds as her gaze traveled past me. I turned to follow it and saw the hotel on the outskirts of town. We were in an industrial area. An area locals worked in but didn't live. No tourists here, either.

We pulled up to the hotel and navigated to an empty parking area off to the side. Elizabeth had pulled out her phone and was reading through the latest messages.

"I've got a room number," she said.

"We're certain it's correct?" I asked.

She shook her head. "Unfortunately, we don't have that kind of confidence in this intel."

"But we're going in anyway."

"Yup."

"Sounds about right." I studied the hotel, scanning windows for signs of anything that stood out. Nothing did.

Elizabeth paid attention to the front of the hotel. Eventually my gaze settled there as well. For ten minutes, no one entered or exited. It was now after one in the afternoon. Those who were departing today had done so. Those slated to arrive would do so in a few hours. The hotel would be humming with cleaning crews, not wandering guests.

The driver, a man about my age named Noah, shifted to the passenger seat where he retrieved a laptop. After inserting a drive of some sort into the USB slot, he pulled up a terminal and began typing away on the keyboard. He slapped the enter key a few times and shifted to face us.

"Security system is ours," he said. "Rear stairwell door is unlocked. Cameras are off."

Elizabeth looked at me. "Ready, Jack?"

"Who's going in?"

"Just us," she said. "He'll stay with Katrine."

A knot formed in my stomach. I didn't like that plan. My only interaction with the guy was him knocking me upside the head. A move he never apologized for. And I still didn't trust Elizabeth, even if she had shown up after the shooting to get us out of there.

"Unless you'd rather her come with us, Jack. But, first, think about the possible consequences. She's not trained as we are. If something goes down, she's a liability. I'm not risking my life to save hers. And if you do, I won't step in to save you."

I leaned forward, making sure Noah was looking me in the eye. "Something happens to her—" I pointed back at Katrine, and then at Elizabeth, "—then something happens to her."

He looked at Elizabeth. Back at me. "You got nothing to worry about, boss. I'm on your side."

"Happy?" Elizabeth asked me.

I nodded and shifted my attention to Katrine. "You stay here. Got it? Stay off your phone. Do not power it back on. If he says you gotta go, then you don't resist. Just go."

"What if something happens to you?" Katrine said.

"Cross that bridge when you reach it," I said. "But not until then. This isn't the kind of place that's gonna do me in. OK?"

She nodded, opened her mouth to say something, but then thought better of it.

I followed Elizabeth out of the van after checking my pistol.

"All good?" she asked.

"All good." I reached the door first, pulled it open, waited for her pass through and followed her in. The air felt warm and still, smelled stale. We paused for a few seconds, listened for footsteps and voices. Neither were present.

She pointed at me, then the stairs. I took the first set with her close behind. After I cleared the landing and next set of steps, she took the lead. We leapfrogged our way up like this until we reached the seventh floor, where we paused once again, this time for longer than a few seconds, to catch our breath.

"I swear this used to be easy," she whispered.

I grinned, nodded, pointed at the door. She reached for the handle and pulled it toward her. I filled the void, keeping my pistol just out of sight as I scanned the hallway in both directions.

Stepping out of the stairwell, I said, "We're good."

The hallway divided into three wings that met in the middle. We were at the far end of one of them. Our destination room was at the far end of another. The best course of action was to clear all three sections in case we had to use the other for an escape.

Elizabeth adjusted her earpiece and said, "We're in. Do you have a visual on the hallway, Noah?" She nodded a few times before gesturing for us to start. "OK. OK. Sounds good."

"What's going on?"

"He's got visuals of the entire floor. We're good to proceed directly to the room."

"How're we getting in? Should we look for someone on the cleaning staff and take their master key?"

"He's got control of the system and can unlock the door from his computer."

"Can I borrow him after this?"

She smirked, looked at me out of the corner of her eye. "You miss this, don't you?"

"Little bit."

"More than the retired life?"

"Tough to say." I heard a door open behind us and checked over my shoulder. No one appeared. "It was nice not having to check behind my back a dozen times an hour, that's for sure. And Mia, you know, I miss her. I've already lost so much time with her. She grows so much in between, and I thought I was there for the long haul this time."

We turned at the corner to the other wing. She slowed the pace. "So, why'd you leave her?"

"Clarissa needed help."

"That's all it took?"

"Maybe I missed the life a little bit."

"Something doesn't jibe. What aren't you telling me, Jack?"

"Plenty." I counted the room numbers in my head and locked in on our destination. "Look, we get through this without you trying to shoot me in the back, or the front, and I'll let you play therapist with me. OK?"

"Deal." She pulled her gun out and inspected it one final time as we stopped two rooms away. "I don't blame you for leaving her. I know there's a lot of loose ends, even if you had a clean slate, whatever that is."

"I'm not even sure anymore. About the clean slate, that is. You're right about the loose ends. And that's part of the reason I accepted their offer. There are things I need to set right before I can spend the rest of my life at a bar on the beach."

She watched me for a few moments, nodding, processing what I had said, presumably. Maybe she'd reached some of the same conclusions I had. This wasn't an easy life to live. And it wasn't easy to give up, either. At some point, you learn to love the excitement. The adrenaline. Even if that comes with always having to check your six in case someone followed you down a dark alley.

"Let's do this," I said.

"One sec." She pressed the comms button and said, "We're ready. All good from your vantage?" She nodded a few times to a response I couldn't hear. "OK. We're moving in."

That was all I needed. The door unlocked with an audible click. I tested the handle with the back of my hand, then opened the door. Elizabeth exploded past me into the room.

"Down! Down! Get down!"

I hurried in behind her, expecting to see someone confused, bouncing foot-to-foot, ready to fight or take off, either through us or out the window.

But the only other person in the room wasn't going to do anything. Not with a hole in his head.

CHAPTER 23

LORRAINE BURST THROUGH THE DOOR TO THE LOADING DOCK expecting to see the same guys standing around smoking cigarettes she'd seen from her room. But no one was out there. On their lunch break, maybe.

Didn't matter.

She scanned the lot for the Tesla tied to her cell phone. It was toward the back, where the superchargers were. She slipped the hoodie over her head, put on her large sunglasses, and hurried to the vehicle. The doors unlocked as she approached. As she went to push the handle to open the door, a car engine revved, tires squealed, and a sedan lurched out of a parking spot.

It had to be about the warehouse and the crypto wallet she took off the man. What else could it be? These guys were enforcers for the organization.

She fumbled the door far enough open for her to squeeze into the driver's seat. She had a few seconds, at most, to get into gear and out of the parking spot.

The other vehicle reached the end of its lane and turned without breaking.

She pinned the accelerator to the floor. The Tesla S Plaid was one of the quickest vehicles in the world zero to sixty. It caught Lorraine by surprise, and she almost skidded into the middle of the road when she braked at the edge of the lot.

In the rearview, she saw the other vehicle coming up fast. It didn't appear they intended to stop. That's one way to do it, she thought. She glanced to her left, spotted one vehicle on approach. It was close, but if she didn't go, the car behind her was guaranteed to collide with her and send her into the road anyway. She yanked the wheel, hit the accelerator, and pulled out in front of the other car, which laid on its horn.

Didn't matter.

She reached sixty in less than three seconds. The other vehicles were far back in her rearview. She wasn't clear yet. The sedan from the lot was in pursuit and making up ground.

Lorraine knew her escape route by heart. Dylan had made her memorize it the moment they arrived. It would be easier to go straight to the motorway, but that would lead anyone in pursuit there as well. There would be no way to lose a competent driver on the highway. The route he planned for her took her through city streets where she might have a chance of shaking her pursuers.

She turned the wheel at the last second and raced down a side street for a block. Then again to the left. A series of lefts and rights followed. Two more to go. Almost there. Now, once she was on the motorway, she'd be in the clear.

A glance in the rearview before she made the next turn revealed a clear path behind her. She wasn't sure when she had lost them. They might be a few feet from making that right, catching her taillights before she disappeared. She kept watch until she completed the turn.

With a sigh she dropped her gaze.

And slammed on the brakes.

"Shit!"

The Tesla decelerated and came to a stop within inches of the barricade. The squealing of the brakes had been loud enough to draw attention from within a small cafe. Two people stepped outside, one hurried over to her. They backed away, almost tripping over their feet, when they saw Lorraine exit the vehicle with a gun in hand.

The high-pitched whine of the other vehicle accelerating far too fast for these narrow streets echoed down the alley.

She looked all around for a hiding spot. Finding nothing promising, Lorraine hurdled the concrete barrier and fled on foot. She heard the other car come to a stop. Doors open. Someone shouted, "Where is she? Where is she?" A lady shrieked in response, perhaps because there was a gun to her face.

Shake it off.

She repeated the thought. There was no time to worry about what was behind her. The next street approached. She sprinted harder. Her legs burned from hips to toes. Her knee felt like it might snap in half. She only had a little further to go. A few more feet. She reached out, let her hand hit the brick wall. The rough brick shredded her skin, leaving it peeled and burning. She bent over, put her hands on her knees, sucked in as much air as she could. Resisting the urge to check around the corner, she forced herself to move again.

"That way." The shouts were distant, drowned out. At first. They grew nearer. Footfalls slapped the asphalt and concrete.

Lorraine inhaled as deeply as she could and took off again. A cramp in her ribs made every step excruciating. The pursuit could go on much longer, so she began scanning for a place to hide. One appeared. A narrow alley between the buildings. She slowed her pace to make the turn.

Tables lined both sides, leaving little space in the lane. Maybe enough for a scooter to pass through. If only one were waiting there for her. More than half the tables were occupied. Two waiters were working outside. She got the attention of one.

"Restroom?" she asked trying not to give away how badly she needed oxygen.

He pointed toward the main restaurant and said, "You must take a table, though."

She looked around. "That one there." Then she jogged over to the restaurant. All eyes were on her. She could feel them. Staring. Judging. For a moment, she slipped back into the girl she used to be and had to remind herself of the woman she had become.

"Yes?" The hostess stepped from behind her stand and blocked Lorraine's path.

"Restroom."

"Only for patrons."

She hiked her thumb over her shoulder. "I have a table out there. Ask the waiter."

"I didn't seat you at that table." She stuck her hand out to further block Lorraine's advance. "You'll need to wait here."

"I don't have time!" Lorraine grabbed the woman's wrist, bent it backward, and tossed her to the floor.

Silverware clanked against plates and chairs grated against the floor as diners panicked or tried to get a better look at what was happening.

Lorraine bulldozed her way through the restaurant, slamming into a waiter and knocking the tray of food to the floor. There was shouting outside, drawing nearer. She heard a man scream in pain. Threats were made. Someone yelled, "She went inside."

By this point, she drove forward on adrenaline alone. The pain dulled. She kept pushing forward. The narrow opening ahead was dimly lit. She grabbed her gun once safely in the hallway. The door was in front of her. She turned and used her back to push it open, surveilling a slice of the restaurant before taking refuge.

Spinning around once inside, her worst fears were realized. There was no way out. Two stalls. A sink. Solid walls. No safe place to hide. No windows. She looked over her shoulder, to her left, at her reflection in the dirty mirror.

"It's been a good ride, babe. Never would've guessed this is how you'd go out."

She dug in her pocket for her cell phone. If this was it, she wanted to tell Dylan how much she appreciated him for pulling her out of the mess her life had become. And how much she hated him for making it even worse. But when it came time to type out the message, she couldn't bring herself to do it. Instead, she wrote, "I want you to know I love you. No matter what happens next." She hit send and stuffed the phone back in her pocket, ignoring the almost instantaneous buzz against her thigh.

Voices rose from outside the ladies' room. One stood out more than the others. A deep voice. Male. Said, "Back here. She's gotta be back here."

She questioned her decision to seek refuge here. Why not the kitchen? Kitchens had exits, right? How else would they take the trash out and hide the cooks coming and going from everyone? She glanced at the mirror again and shook her head. It was a stupid move. But it didn't matter anymore.

There was one benefit to the room. The entrance was maybe two-thirds of the normal size. Only one man could enter at a time.

Someone pounded on the door. She flinched at the sound.

"Fuck you!" she yelled.

The door crashed hard to the floor, knocked from the hinges.

Lorraine had the guy standing there in her sights. But she couldn't pull the trigger.

"Drop the gun! Drop the gun!"

Law enforcement.

"You're OK, lady. We apprehended those men chasing you."

She burst into tears. Adrenaline. Fear. Panic. And finally, relief. Her arm went limp. She dropped to her knees. The gun fell to the floor. The first officer in kicked it away. The next circled behind Lorraine and pulled her feet back, sending her face smacking into the tile. They pulled her arms behind her and placed the cuffs on her.

Weren't they there to rescue her?

"Am I under arrest?"

"Get her out of here," the first guy said, ignoring her.

She yelled at them. "Am I under arrest?"

No one would answer.

As they attempted to force her through the opening, she spread her legs and planted her feet against the wall. A snap of her head and she caught the guy holding her on the bridge of his nose, which crunched audibly. His warm blood mixed in her hair and dampened her scalp. She crashed to the floor, landing hard on her left arm. Pain radiated, then it started to go numb. Had it been broken?

Pain flooded her head, and her vision blurred. She blinked hard until it cleared somewhat. The first officer was standing in front of her, something in his hand aimed at her.

"No," she tried to say. "I don't want to—"

Too late. A hundred and fifty thousand volts of electricity coursed through her body, and she slipped into unconsciousness. The image of the cop smiling at her was the last thing she saw.

CHAPTER 24

THE SUNLIGHT SHONE THROUGH THE GAP IN THE BLINDS AND sliced across the dead man's face as though it were there to pull his soul free from his corpse. I knelt next to him. His skin felt as warm as the living. The only thing I found on him was a flip phone and a metal card with a bunch of numbers etched into it.

"This just happened," I said.

Elizabeth looked over her shoulder from across the room. She had been rifling through dresser drawers. "It looks like they were living out of here. Enough clothes to last a week, minimizing time spent handling laundry."

"You check the fridge?"

She went over to it and pulled the door open. "Let's see, we've got water, beer, some bananas. Not much else." She walked over and knelt on the other side of the body. "That's a nice gunshot wound there."

"No exit hole." I tipped his head to the side so she could see. "Probably a .22. Maybe a .380."

"Nice scratch marks on the back of his neck. Face has a couple splotches, too."

"Definitely a struggle before the fatal shot." I rose and went over to the window, peeled back the curtains, scanned the rear parking lot and loading dock.

Elizabeth joined me by the window. "You think the shooter could have made it here before us, killed this guy, and escaped?"

I played out the scenario from the shooter's point of view and based their actions on how I would've handled the situation. "If it were me back in Bruges, I'd have had an escape route with close turns and a car waiting no more than two streets away. So, depending on where the getaway car was positioned, they could've had a five-minute head start over us. At most. If they drove five miles an hour faster than we did, on average, keeping them within ten of the speed limit, then they'd have spent ten minutes less on the road than us. Assume minimal scouting time, or someone already in place here to watch, then they were up here ten to fourteen minutes prior to our arrival. This wasn't a long struggle. He's not that beat up."

"Maybe this guy got the jump on them. The scratches on the back of the neck could've come from trying to get him off them while he was strangling them."

"One hand on the back of the neck, the other going for a concealed pistol."

Elizabeth nodded as she glanced around the room. "There's no damage anywhere, just a messed-up bed. It wasn't much of a fight. Also, look. The scratches are deep." She wiggled her fingers. "Longer fingernails."

"It was a woman."

Elizabeth nodded. She rose and walked to the other end of the room and went into the bathroom.

I checked the deceased again, this time running my fingers along the guy's back, I found something underneath him. I rolled the guy onto his hip and retrieved the contents on the floor, a folded-up piece of paper.

"What's that?" Elizabeth asked. I hadn't heard her approach.

"Anything in the bathroom?"

"Trash was empty. What did you find on him?"

I unfolded the paper and held it in the sunlight. "It's just a company letterhead."

Her eyebrows lifted. "For what? Where?"

I shook my head, not quite sure what I was looking at. It was a company I had never heard of called Concerted Dynamics. The address was in Denmark.

My mind raced in a million directions at the implications here. Were the people after this woman the same ones trying to kill me? Perhaps she could shed light on who they were and what they wanted with her.

"Jack? What is it?"

I told her the company name, and she pulled it up on her phone.

"I thought that sounded familiar. That's a front company we've traced to the organization that owns that warehouse. They sell security systems, surveillance equipment, comms, probably sell weapons systems, too. Jesus, Jack. What else are these guys into?"

I studied it again, noticed something imprinted on it. "Hang on a sec." I pulled open the nightstand drawer and pulled out the Bible and a pencil. On the desk was a notepad. I set a sheet of it over the receipt and rubbed the pencil lightly over it.

"What did you find?"

"Phone number, maybe. Unmarked account, possibly. Could be a deposit account. A place to leave payment for the real purchase?" I was doing my best to not appear rattled by the revelation. There were more indents. I did the same thing again with the pencil, shading the entire page. Twenty-four words laid out in four columns. A seed phrase for a crypto wallet. I folded both papers up and tucked them away.

Elizabeth snapped a picture of the guy. "Sounds like we need to pay them a visit and see what they know about this guy." She reached for her pocket with one hand, held up a finger on the other as she answered her phone. "Yeah, what've you got, Noah?" She nodded along with the other end of the conversation. "OK, sounds good. Thought we ran into a dead end up here, but Jack's uncovered something we might be able to use."

"What's up?" I asked after she hung up.

"We gotta go. Noah pulled up security footage of the time before we arrived. A Tesla screamed out of the parking lot with another car close behind."

"That's our girl."

"He's already got it tracked. It's a few minutes away."

We sprinted down the stairs. The van was waiting for us. The side door peeled open as we hit the parking lot.

Katrine looked relieved when she saw me. "Everything OK up there? Did you find anything?"

"We've got a few things to look into," I said.

Elizabeth leaned in next to me. "MI6 has a safehouse not far from here. I'm going to see if we can use it. Would be a good place to leave her."

"You think she'll be safe there?" I asked.

"Safer for her there than waiting in the van. We're close to these guys, and I'm fairly certain one of these parties is responsible for her husband's death."

"You mean whoever's responsible for the bomb in Barcelona?"

"Likely, yes. But my guess is he was dead before that." She leaned in closer and whispered, "I think his body was meant to be identified as someone else."

"Van de Berg."

She nodded.

"What makes you think that?" I asked.

She glanced at Katrine for a moment, pulled away from me. "We'll talk about that later."

Noah had navigated through a series of turns and slowed to a stop in front of an alley. "Tesla should be down here."

Elizabeth and I hopped out of the van and walked past the alleyway, holding hands as though we were a couple. Both of us took a quick glance and saw the Tesla in front of a concrete barrier. A forensics van was parked nearby and techs were working inside the car while a couple of uniformed officers watched from a distance.

"Think they've got her?" I asked.

She nodded. "Probably. We'll make sure. But first, let me find out about the safehouse."

We stopped on the other side of the alley. I went inside a market and grabbed a few packs of chorizo and some water for everyone. Elizabeth paced in front of the store, phone to her ear. When I came out, she pressed her lips together and nodded.

"Available?"

"Yeah," she said. "Understaffed, though. We'll have to leave Noah there with her."

"He up to that task?"

"Trust me, you don't want to mess with him, Jack."

"How would he do against a team of assassins?"

"Let's hope we don't have to find out."

CHAPTER 25

THE SAFEHOUSE WAS LOCATED ABOUT FIVE MILES NORTHEAST of the city, close to the water near a town called Edam. Woods surrounded it on three sides. A short, stocky man with an exposed shoulder harness over his cable knit sweater greeted us at the door. He kept his hand on his gun until he had confirmed with his chain of command we were who we said we were.

It was dark inside with all the window shades pulled down. A grid of six televisions lined the wall of the first room on the left. They displayed a mix of news channels and a few grainy security feeds. Some feeds were blank.

The house smelled like bacon, but when I asked, the guy ignored me, and instead told Katrine and Noah where they would stay should they be there overnight.

Elizabeth and I headed outside into the crisp air to talk. The canopy above allowed slices of sunlight to penetrate. A gentle breeze escalated at times and kicked up dead leaves that rustled as they rose and fell. It was the kind of place I could sit and relax half the day. Unfortunately, we didn't have that luxury.

"Are you comfortable with this?" Elizabeth asked. "Leaving her here?"

"As long as the guy watching the house is legit."

"I confirmed he is."

"Should be good to go. What did you mean in the van? About her husband being identified?"

She leaned on the railing and looked out into the woods. "What I'm about to tell you, you can't repeat. Not to anyone, Katrine especially. I need you to promise you won't."

"I won't."

"Not sure I believe you."

"Then don't tell me. I'm sure I'll find out some other way with how this week is going."

"I uncovered a bit about Nev while working this investigation. I'm sure she told you how they were forced out of their business."

I nodded.

"What she didn't know was that him being a degenerate led to their losses more than some criminals taking a cut each week. Those two morons harassing everyone are tied to this same criminal organization. If you didn't push for them, then you paid. Nev got in wrong with them and bled the business dry while never really making a dent in what he owed, because he'd dig himself further down. From what we gather, he told them he was coming into some money. Then he disappeared."

I wondered if Katrine knew of this. She didn't have a high opinion of Nev, and it sounded like she hadn't for some time. This would explain it.

Elizabeth continued, "He didn't leave over a woman. He left for a job, and ultimately, he was sacrificed and placed in that building. We just don't know precisely why."

"How'd you find this out?"

"I've got my sources. But, first, take a look at this." She swiped on her phone a few times then showed me a picture of a man with dark hair wearing a brown leather jacket. "This is Nev." She pulled the phone back and brought up another picture. "Look at this."

Again, dark hair, leather jacket. Onboard a boat in a marina. "Where is he in that photo?"

"Nev? No clue, because that's not him."

"You're kidding. They could be twins." I studied the picture harder, zoomed in on his face. There, I could see some differences, but not too much.

"That's Dylan Van de Berg. The one who tried to kill you in Luxembourg, and I'm certain he was the one who was in Bruges today. I'm not sure how he and Nev hooked up, but my intel says they were both in Barcelona at the same time. Right around the time of the explosion in that building. This woman is the key to it all. I know she is, Jack. We can't screw this up. If Van de Berg isn't aware she's been detained, he might show up at the hotel."

"So, we use her as bait?"

Elizabeth shrugged. "We have to get her first."

"What's the plan?"

"They are preparing MI6 credentials for us. This guy here can print and laminate them. It'll get us into the police station. Noah is working on the woman. We need her name and any alias if she has one. I'm assuming she does based on the other intel we have."

"We gonna bring her back here?"

"I think that's the best plan. They've got reinforced rooms in the basement. We can interrogate her down there. Noah can get her fingerprints. He's got a couple of databases he can check. We can pass it along to MI6, too, but there's risk there."

"If they want her, they'll take her."

She nodded. "They're not looking to get involved, Jack. But if we ask for further help, they'll want to know what we know. And you know how these agencies can work. We might not get anything in return from them."

"We only need to know who she's working with and who might be after her. If she'll give that up, I think we can hand her over to MI6 and let them dig in on her."

"If she'll give it up." Elizabeth bent over and scooped up some dirt and debris. She shook it in her hand, then threw it like she was skipping a stone across calm lake water. "You saw what she did in that room. From what we can gather, the police didn't apprehend her where she left the car. She ran. Fought them in a restaurant bathroom where they had her cornered. They had to tase her to get her under control."

"Police didn't follow her from the hotel. Someone else had the jump on us finding her."

"No, but that doesn't change the fact they apprehended her and what she did up to that point."

"Survival instinct. That's all. We get her out of there and bring her to a place like this, she'll understand that the rules don't apply. One of us goes to work on her, the other acts kind and then flips. She'll roll over and give up the shooter."

"You think she knows the shooter's true identity?"

"Guess that depends on their relationship. Is she just an asset? If so, then doubtful. But..." I turned toward the sound of a snapping branch and waited a beat. There was no one there I could see. Could've been an animal. "You saw the hotel room. A man was staying there as well."

She nodded. "Yeah, shaver in the bathroom, two toothbrushes."

"Men's clothing in the drawers."

"They're more than partners. They're lovers."

"Let's hope it's a one-sided relationship." I turned to face her.

"Meaning?"

"They're not Bonnie and Clyde. He's keeping her there against her will, somehow. I mean, she could leave, but he's got something on her to keep her there."

"And if they are Bonnie and Clyde?"

"Let's rewrite the ending of the story."

CHAPTER 26

WE SAT IN THE VAN, PARKED OUTSIDE OF THE POLICE STATION. The sun was setting, washing the neighborhood with a purplish hue. A few officers lingered outside the front door. They were talking with a man and woman in plain clothes. The guy had a black eye. The woman had been crying.

On the way over, we stopped and bought a change of clothes, something more suited for our cover. The guy at the house supplied us each with a credpack. Elizabeth's was easier, already in the system. They used another agent's creds for mine. He was on administrative leave, the type only those inside Legoland, MI6's headquarters, would know about. He also supplied us with handcuffs, service pistols, and windbreakers.

"What else do you know about this woman?" I asked.

"There's very little available on her. Name is Lorraine Chaput. Pretty much a loner. Got into some trouble and received court-mandated therapy and probation. She made it through probation, but never finished the therapy. Dropped off the radar until now."

"Charges?"

"Then, or now?"

"Now."

"They detained her in the restaurant. They wanted to sort everything out as she resisted them, plus there were the other men who had been chasing her. The one the police caught gave some ridiculous story. He's probably waiting for a call to come in to spring him free. Shortly after bringing her in, the body was discovered in her room."

"They might not be so keen on giving her up."

"Once the directive comes through from headquarters, they won't have much choice."

"Hard to believe it'll be that simple."

She shrugged, then opened the door. "Let's go find out. But first, you *can* speak with an English accent, right?"

I laughed. "I'm kinda like Kevin Costner in *Robin Hood*. Might be best to stick with an American accent."

"Say bottle."

I tried. She asked me to repeat it, slower, after demonstrating. Finally, she said, "OK, maybe you should remain quiet."

Burned coffee lingered in the air. We stood in front of the reception desk. An officer in the distance lifted a finger and went back to her paperwork. The silence in the room made it feel like we were waiting to check into a hotel after everyone had gone to bed if not for the occasional chatter over the radio.

The officer came over and said, "Help you two?" She picked up on the fact we weren't local.

"You've detained Lorraine Chaput," Elizabeth said. "She's a suspect in a case we're working. We have a directive here for you to release her into our custody." She set the paperwork on the desk.

The officer retrieved it and looked it over. "I'm going to have to speak to someone about this. Hold on, please." She pointed at the bank of seats bolted to the floor.

"Got fresh coffee?" I asked. I could sense Elizabeth rolling her eyes, but I thought the accent was pretty good.

She pointed at the pot next to the seats.

I said, "Fresh."

"Hold on," she huffed at me. With the paper in hand, she disappeared behind a door, returning a minute later with a Styrofoam cup full of coffee. She left it on the counter, then walked away again.

"How's that?" Elizabeth pointed at the cup as I took a seat next to her.

I took a sip and wanted to spit it out. "It'll do, I guess. Not much choice, is there?"

"Could get something after."

"I'll just make some when we get back to the house. Gonna need it. Got a feeling we'll be up with Lorraine most of the night."

The officer came through the door, pushing it a bit too hard and sending it into the wall. It slapped with a thud and then swung back, bouncing off her hip before closing. She pressed a button, and we heard a buzz. She lifted a section of the counter and walked over to us.

"Can I see your IDs?"

Elizabeth handed hers over first. The officer studied it, looked back and forth between the picture and the woman seated in front of her. She handed it back and took mine. She seemed to spend more time reviewing it. At least, longer than I'd have liked.

"Name?" she asked.

I repeated all the details on the card: name, address, ID number, blood type, organ donor status.

"OK, OK," she said, handing me the card. "Follow me."

She led us down a hallway lit with fluorescent lights. They cast a yellow tint over everything. We turned and went down a shorter hall with two doors on either side. Windows were fixed in the middle of the doors from waist to head height. I looked past the officer and saw a blonde woman seated against the back wall, her hair covering part of her face.

The officer gestured to the window. "That her?"

Elizabeth scooted in, took a moment, said, "Yes."

The officer unlocked the door. She blocked me and told Elizabeth, "Go confirm."

The door fell shut behind Elizabeth. The woman looked up, brushed her hair out of her face. She nodded. Twice. Sighed. Stood. Elizabeth looked over her shoulder and gave a nod, tight and terse.

Less than three minutes later, we were standing outside. The wind had shifted, coming in strong from the north. The air tasted of salt. Clouds gathered overhead, reflecting the final traces of the setting sun.

I slid the van door open and gestured for Lorraine to enter. She hadn't spoken up to this point, and we hadn't asked her a single question. Once she was seated and the door had been closed, she was ready to sing.

"I'll tell you everything I know if you'll let me walk free."

CHAPTER 27

DYLAN STOOD IN THE WOODS BEHIND THE HOUSE A FEW MILES away from Amsterdam, near the coast. The sun had dipped almost to the horizon behind him. It cut through the woods like thousands of tiny lasers. Anyone looking toward his position would be blinded.

He marked his arm with a sharpie each time he spotted someone. So far, he had two marks. Two men, one short and stocky, the other a bit bigger. Never together.

Darkness swept over the area in a matter of seconds as the sun's rays no longer penetrated the woods. Dylan tucked the scope in his bag and readied himself to move. From the same bag, he retrieved the Glock 17. His hand brushed against a cold, metal cylinder. He threaded the suppressor on the end of the barrel. On his waistband, he placed a spare magazine in a holster. In his right boot, he had a spare knife should things not go well. He doubted he'd have to use it.

Fifty yards without cover separated Dylan from the house. He decided to approach diagonally, which afforded him a view of the back, side yard, and the end of the driveway. He kept low to the ground and traveled on a straight path. From his vantage point in the woods, he spotted the trip-wires as they reflected the setting sun. As he neared the location, he stopped, pulled out his flashlight and slipped the red lens cover over it.

The muted light would be difficult to spot from inside unless someone was staring directly at him.

He cleared the inner and outer tripwire and made his final sprint toward the house, stopping at the corner to rest and collect himself until the silence overpowered the gaps between his breaths.

Clouds gathered overhead, blocking any remaining light. He pulled out his flashlight with the lens cover still on it and inspected the roof overhang. From a distance, it had appeared there were no security cameras, and now he had confirmed it. Perhaps they thought the tripwire was enough. Or maybe he'd triggered another detection method he hadn't spotted.

A light flipped on and illuminated a good portion of the rear deck. Dylan pressed against the wall and listened. He heard the flicking of a lighter. The smell of a burning cigarette reached him a few seconds later. With his pistol at the ready, he eased around the corner of the house and saw the short, stocky man leaning over the railing with a cigarette hanging from his fingers.

Too easy.

He lined up his shot and squeezed the trigger twice. Both hit center mass within millimeters of each other. The guy fell forward and flipped over the deck railing.

Dylan moved up the stairs deftly like a lynx, scanning the facade up to the roof. He spotted the first camera and chastised himself for missing it while in the woods. It was easy to gloss over, even at this distance, and he wondered if he were wrong about the side of the house. It hadn't mattered, apparently.

Rather than verifying the man he'd shot was dead, Dylan stopped next to the sliding glass door and waited for a moment. The guy had left it open a few inches. Whatever was on the stove rode the warm air into the cold. It was quiet, though.

He inched his way forward until he had a view inside. Every step exposed more of the main level. He gripped the door handle and slid it toward him until it was open wide enough for him to slip through.

The room was as wide as the house, comprised of the kitchen, an eating area, and a living area where two couches faced each other, a coffee table in the middle, a television mounted on the wall. A hallway in the middle of the room led to the front door. Stairs on the left. Another room on the right. The light from that room flickered into the dim hallway.

He crept toward the stairwell and that room, which had a wide-cased opening. There were two chairs and six televisions mounted on the wall. Some had the news on. Others had security feeds. Some were blank. Maybe the guy he'd shot was too interested in his cell phone and his next cigarette break to pay attention.

Dylan worked his way up the stairs, keeping his footfalls along the outer edges of the steps to prevent alerting anyone to his presence. He'd made it halfway when another man opened the door at the top of the stairs. The guy stood there, stunned, processing Dylan and trying to place him.

"The fu—"

Dylan didn't give him time to finish. He squeezed the trigger. The bullet hit the guy in the stomach. The guy stumbled back and fell into the room he had left moments ago. He was now out of sight.

Not good. What if someone else was in there? Dylan took the remaining stairs two at a time, the Glock remained aimed ahead. At the top of the stairs, he cleared both ends of the hallway then turned his attention to the man on the floor. The guy was using his elbows to pull himself farther into the room.

Without hesitation, Dylan planted three more rounds into the guy. It wasn't enough to end his life then and there. He continued to scoot back, even with blood dribbling from his mouth and leaking from four bullet wounds.

Dylan walked into the room, leading with his pistol, scanning for any other threats. There were none.

"P-p-please." The guy held a bloodied hand out.

"Sorry, mate." Dylan put one final round through the man's forehead and turned away, not waiting to absorb the man's final moments.

Every doorway in the hall was closed. He started at the left end and methodically cleared each room until he'd reached the final one. He waited, pressed his ear to the door, listened for signs of life. He recognized the song playing as an old tune from The Mamas & The Papas. A song he'd heard plenty of times before as a kid.

He reached for the knob, found it unlocked. He turned it slowly, pushed the door open until he saw her stretched out on the bed.

She looked up.

He made his entry.

She gasped.

He smiled, lowered his pistol.

Tears spilled over her eyelids. "Dylan? What are you doing here?"

He smiled. "Surprised?"

She glanced around the room. He followed her gaze, knowing she was looking for a weapon. She threw her phone at him. An odd choice. He dodged the phone and moved forward. Her expression changed from shock to anger. She leapt off the bed and grabbed the lamp on the night-stand, ripping it free from the wall. Then she lunged and reached him faster than he had anticipated.

One arm was occupied trying to holster his pistol. The other went up to deflect the blow. But the lamp was solid metal, heavy, and he hoped the bone hadn't snapped upon impact.

With the pistol in hand, he retaliated, catching her on the side of the head with the Glock. She grunted and stumbled back but didn't go down. He saw to it that she did by delivering another strike to her head. She fell to the side onto the bed. Blood dribbled across her face and settled onto the white sheets.

"The hell were you thinking, Katrine?"

Her eyelids fluttered, held open for a few seconds, then slammed shut.

He grimaced when he tried to move his left hand. He looked down and saw how swollen his forearm was. Could've been worse, he figured. This was a bone bruise, at best. Small fracture, at worst. He had to give it to her, she tried. Which was more than his worthless cousin Nev had done.

Katrine moaned and turned her head. She stared at him in disbelief. "Why?"

"Why not?"

She tried to shake her head, winced, closed her eyes again.

Dylan looked back for her phone and grabbed it off the floor. He powered it down. Placed it in his pocket. Then he pulled the unconscious woman off the bed and hoisted her over his shoulder.

Less than five minutes later, he was loading her into the trunk of his car.

CHAPTER 28

ELIZABETH CUT THE LIGHTS ON THE VAN WHEN WE WERE A quarter-mile from the safehouse. With the GPS zoomed in, she managed to navigate the road in the pitch black. For a brief moment, rain had started coming down, splattering against the windshield and reducing visibility even further.

We'd decided to wait until we were at the house to begin interrogating Lorraine. She sat in the row behind us with her knees pulled to her chest and her face buried in her arms. It'd been quite a day for the woman. Wouldn't be surprised if she had passed out from exhaustion. Had that been the reason she had said she was ready to talk so soon? Since getting into the van, she hadn't said a word. We hadn't pried, either.

Elizabeth said little on the drive back. Any attempts to engage her in conversation had been met with a word or two in response and nothing more. Guess we were all feeling a bit drained. Life had been upended.

I wondered how Katrine was doing in the house. She missed Bernie, that was certain. But of everyone involved, her life had been pulled apart the most in the past twenty-four hours. From confirmation of her husband's death to the shooting this morning, and now three hours from home, she was holing up in an MI6 safehouse. I chose this life. Elizabeth did, as well. Even our new friend, Lorraine, had taken steps to get her where she was today.

But not Katrine.

The GPS indicated the driveway was coming up fast. Elizabeth let her foot off the gas until the van rolled along at a snail's pace. I understood the reasoning—we didn't want the brake lights giving us away. But every second that passed caused my anxiety to ratchet up a notch. I was eager to begin interrogating Lorraine and unlocking the secret behind this whole mess.

Since the moment we had her in our custody, I'd been wanting to reach out to Clarissa to see what intel she could feed us. In the end, I figured it was better to wait. If she or Beck had a use for the woman, they'd try to intercept her from us. I didn't put it past them tracking me somehow. And I hadn't made any effort to ditch the phone or swap out the SIM for use outside of the house in Bruges.

A mistake?

Possibly.

I also wanted to know if they'd show up. How closely were they watching me? If at all?

Since leaving Bruges, I hadn't heard a peep from her. Perhaps they were waiting to see where I settled in for more than an hour or two. For all the energy I would put into Lorraine, I had to match it to remain aware and anticipate the counter from another party. Whether that was Clarissa and Beck, I'd find out soon enough. I was sure of that.

The van left asphalt and rolled along the driveway. Gravel crunched under the tire. A few errant pieces kicked up and pinged off the underside of the van. We might as well have had the lights on high. I scanned the woods off to the side. Saw nothing.

"Shit."

I turned toward Elizabeth. Her lips were parted. Her head shook.

"Shit," she said again.

The front door was open wide. Light spilled out in a cone, washed over the walkway and faded into the grass.

Before the van had stopped, I had my door open, pistol in hand. I hopped out and sprinted to the front of the house. I gazed out over the property. Within a few seconds, my eyes adjusted to the low light stretching to the street. The rain stopped. Nothing else moved.

The van lurched and groaned as though Elizabeth had thrown it in park prior to coming to a stop. She dashed from the driver's seat to my location, pistol drawn.

"Ready?" I said.

"What about her?" She pointed at the van. Lorraine stood between the front seats and leaned over the dashboard.

I looked up. "Someone could be up there, waiting for us to move into their sights."

"You go," she said. "I'll watch her."

"No. We go in together. It's not safe otherwise."

Elizabeth bit her bottom lip and bounced on her feet. "OK, OK. Let's secure her and then we'll roll."

After binding Lorraine's wrists with zip ties, we entered the house in tactical formation, clearing each room on the main floor. It was empty and looked undisturbed. But a glance through the rear glass door revealed something. Blood smeared on the deck railing.

"Looks like one down outside." I turned away.

Elizabeth shook her head. "Not getting a good feeling about this."

"Join the club." I moved past her. "Let's go upstairs."

I led the way, taking the stairs slowly until we reached the top. Elizabeth backed me up as I dashed across the hallway to reach Noah, who was on the floor. It didn't take long to confirm he was deceased.

Elizabeth's face darkened, and her eyes misted over. "I'm sorry, Noah. I'm so sorry." She looked at me, and I thought for a moment she was going to lose it.

"Gonna be OK?"

"No, but I'll deal with it later."

The door to Katrine's room was wide open. There was blood on the carpet. I steadied myself for what was to come. In the short time I'd known the woman, I'd developed an affinity for her. She had a confidence and a kindness to her. She didn't deserve to die like this.

"You want me to take it?" Elizabeth asked.

"No, I got this." I stepped into the room and took in the scene. The blood-stained sheets. The heavy lamp on the floor. A few things strewn about from the dresser, none of it Katrine's. "She's not here."

"Jack, look at this."

I left the room and met Elizabeth near the stairs where she crouched and shone her phone's flashlight on a section of carpet. She panned around, revealing several drops of blood on the dark hardwoods. It was concentrated in one area. Perhaps she had reached this spot on her own or had been hit here. There were only a few other drops on the stairs. We found a few more leading to the back door.

"We need to verify the guard's dead," I said. I had no doubt he was.

Elizabeth followed me out on the deck. She covered the area while I leaned over the railing. His body was crumpled on the ground, face down.

"I should call this in," she said.

"Let's get out of here first," I said. "We don't need to get bogged down with them questioning us."

"They're going to want to."

"I get that. Let them do it after we've got Lorraine someplace safe."

I left the deck and walked around the side of the house. Stopping and listening. The quiet was interrupted by the sound of a car engine revving.

"We might have company," I called out.

Elizabeth sprinted to my side. In between breaths, she said, "What's wrong?"

"Just heard a car."

"Was it close?"

"Closer than I'd like—"

Something cracked close by. We both turned toward the sound. It was too loud to be someone stepping on a branch. Then we heard the van door slam.

"Lorraine," Elizabeth said.

We sprinted to the front yard. Lorraine was a few feet from the van, on her stomach. Somehow, she'd managed to get her hands in front of her. She pushed up, got a foot under her, then the other, began running. Elizabeth dashed after her. They slipped past the light the house offered, and I lost them in the dark.

I ran to the van. The door hung open. I leaned in, opened the glove box and pulled out a large flashlight. Then I started in the direction the women had gone. A hundred yards or so later, I found them wrestling for control over each other.

"All right, that's enough, Lorraine," I said.

They didn't stop. I swung the light across the ground and spotted Elizabeth's pistol. It was far enough away we didn't have to worry about it. I tucked my own in its holster and pulled the women apart. Lorraine dug her fingernails into my neck as she turned into me and attempted a choke-hold, the only thing she could do with her wrists bound. I countered her movements, and within ten seconds had her neutralized and unable to wriggle free.

Elizabeth scooped up the flashlight and shone it in a circle, landing on me.

"You OK?" she said.

"Yeah. Your gun's over there." I jutted my chin to the right. She followed with the flashlight. "We still have those restraints in the van. Go get them." For the next thirty seconds I kept Lorraine pinned down. I'd worked my way up to a kneeling position, my knee in the middle of her back. "The hell were you thinking. Police will be all over you."

"I'd rather take my chances with them than a couple of spooks."

"Gonna let you in on a secret." I leaned in a few inches from her ear. "We're both retired spooks. That means we don't have to adhere to any rules."

"Screw you." She turned her head and tried to spit at me, but it missed the mark. "I know who you are."

"Got them." Katrine fixed the rubber handcuffs to the woman's wrists and held her in place while I stood. I yanked Lorraine off the ground and led her back to the van.

"What do you want?" Lorraine said after we had her restrained in the van. "For Christ's sake, I only did what he made do."

"Who?" Elizabeth asked. "Who are you working for?"

"Working for?" Lorraine forced a laugh. "It's more complicated than that. I owe him everything." She glanced to the side and clenched her teeth. "And nothing."

CHAPTER 29

THE BANGING IN THE TRUNK LASTED TEN MINUTES BEFORE the sedative kicked in and rendered Katrine unconscious. Perhaps Dylan should've killed her at the house and waited there for Noble to return. Time was short, though. Lorraine's situation could prove dire and unwind everything he'd work to build. Kidnapping Katrine was the best option at hand. With her in his possession as a bargaining chip, he could get Noble to the table to *negotiate*.

Now there were two stops to make. The first was risky. The second had the potential to get him killed. Or worse...apprehended. He shuddered at the thought of life in prison.

He parked the car at the far end of the street after passing the old apartment twice. They had abandoned it in favor of the hotel a few weeks ago after receiving an anonymous tip they were closing in on him. They, of course, had no names and no affiliations. The tip could've been bullshit. One of his agency contacts who wanted to screw with him, so they sent a confidential informant to his door with a made-up story. To his credit, the possible CI was pretty convincing. It wasn't a long walk to imagine that the people he'd stolen the digital wallet containing the Bitcoin from would be after him.

He and Lorraine had each packed a carry-on sized suitcase and a backpack and left that night. He hadn't returned, not even to outfit a camera on the rooftop across the street.

He removed and re-threaded the suppressor to the Glock and swapped out the magazine for a full one. Seventeen rounds in the mag, plus one in the chamber. If he had to use them all, then it would be, by definition, a bad night.

The route taken was not direct. He walked down the perpendicular street to the north. Halfway down the block was an alley that cut behind his building. Hidden under a pile of pallets was a descending stairway that led to the boiler room. It was hot, very much in stark contrast to the cold and damp outside.

Dylan could walk the route blindfolded. He and Lorraine had spent enough time wandering the building in all conditions, night, day, drunk, drugged, so they could escape in any and all conditions.

Though there was an elevator that traveled from the basement to the rooftop, he opted for the stairs. Each floor had a thick steel door with a narrow window that ran from the middle to the top. Enough for him to procure a view of the entire floor. Dylan bounded up the stairs two or three at a time until he reached the landing for the sixth floor. He took a moment to catch his breath, then double-checked his handgun again, ensuring the magazine was seated properly and the suppressor threaded correctly.

He could tell when he reached the apartment that it had been breached. The tip had paid off. Someone had been looking out for him, after all. The hair that had been wound around the doorknob and set in a small cut in the frame was broken in half, blowing in the stream of warm air pouring out of the overhead vent. He checked the knob. Unlocked.

He took a few moments to compose himself, breathing in for four beats, hold for four beats, out for four beats. Three repetitions, and his heart rate had settled. His breaths were long, deep, and steady now. His focus unwavering.

The door opened with ease and swung to the wall where it settled as though a magnet were fixed to it. There were dishes piled in the sink. Pizza boxes piled on the counter. It smelled like garbage.

Dylan stepped in. A column offered cover, and he took it. From there, he eased to the right until he had a view of the living area and the man sitting on the sofa, his back to Dylan. A few more steps and he had the guy.

"Don't move." Dylan tapped the guy on the head with the end of the suppressor and took a step back. "I want to see your hands. Now."

The guy lifted his arms up, his left traveling higher than the right.

"All the way," Dylan said.

The guy twisted and turned his head. "Look, I'm just—"

"Shut up. Lean forward."

The guy leaned forward.

"Hands behind your head."

The guy wrapped both of his meaty hooks behind his cranium and placed his right over his left.

"Now stand."

The man grunted and rocked back and forth, finally getting to his feet after a few tries. He had a bit of a middle-aged gut but looked in shape otherwise.

"Turn around."

They were now face to face, only the couch separating them. Dylan studied him for a few moments in an attempt to place the guy's face. He couldn't.

"Who do you work for?"

"You know who."

"I wouldn't have asked if I did."

"You two have been sloppy lately. I hear your girlfriend landed in jail today, too. Only a matter of time before—"

Dylan had had enough. He pulled the trigger and placed a bullet in the guy's lower abdomen. The man let out a hollow groan and stumbled forward. One hand on his gut, the other on the couch. He looked to his left. Dylan followed the man's gaze and saw his gun on the end table.

"Don't even think about it," Dylan said. "Pretty stupid to leave it there, wasn't it?"

The color drained from the guy's face. "Help me."

"You've got maybe thirty minutes left if you receive no medical attention. Now, I've got no contract on you, so other than the fact you're here waiting to see if I show up so you can kill me, I've got no reason to want you dead. And I think your current predicament will preclude you from trying to come after me. So, why don't you help me out, and then I'll get the ambulance dispatched."

The man nodded as he went to a knee on the couch. He huddled forward, his head resting on the seat back. "What do you want to know?"

"Who the fuck do you work for?"

"They'll kill me if I say."

Dylan slapped the guy over the head with his pistol. "Are you goddamn stupid, man? I'm going to kill you if you don't. You're halfway there already. I can simply leave, and you'll die a slow, painful death here. Do you want to be saved or not?"

The guy lurched upward. He'd slid his hand inside his coat. Dylan's focus dialed in on the movement. Time slowed. Millimeter by millimeter, he saw the man pulling his hand free.

He's going to shoot me.

All Dylan had to do was aim upward slightly, and he'd place a bullet in the man's heart.

So, he did.

The guy's eyes widened in the moment between Dylan squeezing the trigger and the ensuing muzzle blast. The impact sent the guy flailing backward, tripping over himself and crashing to the floor. His hand, now free from inside his coat, opened as his arm fell to the side. A piece of paper dropped from his grip.

He had no weapon.

Dylan groaned. If he'd have waited another second, he would've seen the man was offering information and not trying to kill him. Oh well. Dylan wasn't going to let him live anyway. But who knew what information had died with the guy.

He stepped around the couch, grabbed the paper and unfolded it. There was a word and number starting with thirty-three written on it. The number was a French phone number. The name was gibberish. A code word, perhaps. He'd worry about it later. First, he had to retrieve his belongings and then get to the police station before someone else returned to the apartment and found their associate dead.

CHAPTER 30

ELIZABETH GRABBED THE COMPUTER FROM THE SECURITY system before we left the house and studied the footage for most of the drive back to Amsterdam. It didn't take long for her to find footage of Van de Berg. Now her aim was to turn it into something we could use.

I found a motel a couple miles north of the city. The kind of place where no one would ask questions. The half-hour drive had left Lorraine subdued, and she didn't act up when we removed the cuffs. Presumably she realized if we were going to kill her, we'd have added her to the pile of bodies at the house. She now refused to go into any more detail about her involvement with the man who had taken Katrine.

How would she react to a cleaned-up picture of him from the surveillance footage? That could be a tell as to their relationship. Would she try to protect him? Or save herself?

"How's it going?" I asked Elizabeth, who was hunched over the laptop on the far side of one of beds.

"I'm getting there. This isn't my forte, though. Noah would have had this done in two minutes." She bit down hard and fought off the tears.

"Got someone back in London that can do it?"

She sighed and shook her head. "I mean, yeah, I do, but...there's already such a mess to report at that house. I want to finish this first, because after they find out their man's dead because of me, I'm gonna be in some serious trouble."

"It's not all you," I said. "I'm part of this."

She looked up and smiled. "Appreciate that, Jack. You owe me nothing. Them arresting you will do more harm than good. I can assure you of that." She returned her attention to the screen.

"Gonna go for a walk. You good with her?" I pointed at Lorraine, who was faking sleep.

Elizabeth nodded.

"All right, watch her. She's faking now, might be planning something."

"I'm not planning anything," Lorraine said. "Trying to clear my mind, is all. It's called meditation. You should try it, Jack."

"Right. Unfortunately, it takes the edge off the anxiety, and I think that's what's kept me alive all these years." I leaned in closer to Elizabeth. "I've got my phone. Call me if you need anything."

She looked up from the small screen and blinked me into focus. "Where're you going?"

"Saw a little store up the road. Gonna grab a few things."

I stepped out onto the exposed walkway. The wind gusted heavily from the north. The clouds hid the sky and reflected the light from the city. Was the rain earlier a teaser? Were we in for a winter storm?

I kept to the side of the road, only stepping onto the wet ground when a vehicle approached. I tried to relax my mind, but the same question kept popping up. How did I get into this mess? Things had snowballed so quickly since arriving in Bruges. And since leaving, I hadn't heard a word from Clarissa. Odd, for sure, considering all that had happened today. I pulled out the cell she had provided and checked my messages and calls. None.

Logic said I had been the target at the breakfast place in Bruges. But recent actions suggested otherwise. What did Van de Berg want with Katrine? And what was the relationship between him and Lorraine? They worked together, but were they partners in other ways, too?

Concern for Katrine gnawed at my gut. The only way around it was to confront all the possibilities. If the guy wanted her dead, he'd have killed her at the house. No point in dragging her around. She was a liability in everything he did now. Perhaps he planned on using her as a bargaining chip. I'd get a call from him, and he'd want to exchange Katrine for Lorraine. Fine with me. In fact, if I could arrange it, I would do it right now. I had no way of reaching him, though.

Could there be more to the story? Hard to say, but experience said yes. I only had a limited number of facts. Facts that were given to me by others. There were few reasons to hold someone hostage. And none of them were good.

I hustled the last hundred yards or so to the store. The place was deserted, save for the employees and a younger couple lingering by the frozen foods who looked pretty strung-out. I grabbed water, snacks, a notebook and pen, and a few toiletries. Behind the register, they had a selection of pay-as-you-go cell phones. I bought two, figuring Elizabeth and I could use them to communicate if we needed to separate.

After leaving, I checked the phone Clarissa had given me again. No messages. No calls. Something was off. I walked toward a light on the outside of the building and set up my burner. Called Clarissa.

She answered on the fourth ring. "Hello?" There was a tightness to her voice. "Who is this?"

"It's me."

"Thank God. I've been worried sick all day. Jack, you've gotta get out of Bruges."

"Way ahead of you." I monitored a car that pulled up. The people that got out looked like friends of the junkies inside.

"What's that mean? If you're not in Bruges, where are you?"

"Rather not say. Why are you glad I'm not there?"

"I guess you know. There was a hit planned and executed on you this morning. And then we got word a team was en route to Bruges to clean up. We're just not sure who the cleaners are working for."

"Thanks for confirming. I was there." I debated telling her about Katrine's situation and how Elizabeth and I apprehended Lorraine. Clarissa might have intel we could use. Or her digging in might lead someone right to us. "When did you find out about the hit?"

"About a half-hour prior."

"Why didn't you call or text?"

"Are you kidding? I did. I've been texting and calling you all day. I thought...I don't even want to say it. You haven't received any of them?"

I pulled the phone out again and opened up the call and text histories. "Staring at it right now. There's nothing there."

"Oh no." She muffled the phone and said something I couldn't quite make out. "You need to get out of there now. Someone intercepted the SIM. They've seen everything I've sent you. They must be tracking you by the phone."

Distant headlights felt like threats. The junkies lingering in front of the store looked like a hit team.

"You there?" Clarissa said.

"Yeah. Feels like the world's closing in on me, though."

"Where are you?"

"I don't feel safe telling you over the phone." I glanced all around me. "Clarissa, if someone was able to gain that kind of access to the phone, they had to know you gave it to me. Right?"

"I can't think of another explanation."

"Other than Beck—"

"I know what you're thinking," she interrupted. "It's not him, Jack. I can promise you that."

"What if they're monitoring you now?"

She cursed. "Good point. Get rid of the phones. I'm going to give you a dial-in to use next that'll make the call route through Siberia if you need to reach me again. But try to call from a public phone."

I committed the number to memory and wrote a version in code in the notebook. "I'll be in touch soon."

After hanging up, I started to dismantle the phone Clarissa had given me. I stopped right before snapping the SIM card. I was tired of running. Tired of guessing who was after me. If they really wanted me, they'd find me through the phone. I just had to sit and wait.

But to do so, I had to get back to the motel before anyone else.

CHAPTER 31

DYLAN ENTERED THE POLICE STATION DRESSED IN DARK JEANS, a button up shirt, and a blazer. He wore his fake DSGE credentials on his neck on a lanyard. The few cops lingering about glanced his way, nodded as though they were fraternal brothers, then went about their business.

He walked up to the desk and waited for the woman to acknowledge him. It took a few minutes, and he waited patiently for it. She stood with a huff. Stared him down. Then finally made her way over.

She spoke in Dutch. "Help you?"

He replied in French. "I need to see about a woman you apprehended today."

She replied in French. "Let me guess, Lorraine Chaput."

He tried to conceal his wince but failed. She lifted an eyebrow. "How'd you guess?" he asked.

She pointed at his lanyard. "Some other agents were in here not too long ago. They took her."

He slowed his breathing for a few cycles, then said, "Who?"

"You know I can't tell you that."

"Can you tell me which agency they were with? Was it local?"

She leaned forward and he couldn't help but notice how her breasts swallowed the center of her shirt. She whispered, "Couple of Brits. MI6. I can't say anything more than that."

He turned and headed for the door.

"Do you want to leave a number with me? I can call if she turns back up."

"Sure." He called out a number that would route to a message service, though he figured it was a long shot.

Outside, anger and rage rose like bile in Dylan over the revelation that MI6 had come to collect Lorraine just a short time before him. Of course, he knew it wasn't MI6. The pieces were laid out before him and the puzzle was practically put together. This had Noble written all over it. And he had an accomplice.

Once inside his vehicle, he screamed. "How could this happen?" Lorraine's sloppiness had started when she began talking about them running away, starting a family. Now it had led to this.

His tantrum had roused his prisoner in the trunk. Katrine banged on the lid and kicked the rear seat.

"I'll fucking shoot you if you knock that seat down."

He knew she couldn't reply, not with a gag in her mouth. She also couldn't do much if she managed to break the seat latch. Her wrists and ankles were bound.

Dylan felt uncomfortable waiting in the parking lot of a police station any longer. He left and drove toward the motorway. Before he reached the onramp, his phone rang. He answered and pulled onto the first side street he came to.

The guy on the other end said, "What's going on?"

Dylan said, "Lorraine is gone."

"How?"

"They told me MI6 came to collect her."

"Hold on." The man on the other end tapped his keyboard several times. Came back on and said, "Bullshit. MI6 has nothing to do with her."

"Noble. I'm sure of it. And some freelancer. Not sure who. I only saw him and Katrine in Bruges." He turned the key in the ignition. "Someone got them out. Can you track Noble again?"

"Haven't been able to since this morning. Someone interfered. Blocked any transmission to that phone he was using."

"Dammit."

"Give me a few minutes. I'm gonna try something. Call you back."

Dylan exited the vehicle. At the rear of the car, he popped the trunk. Katrine blinked several times then shook him into focus. She stared wide-eyed. Panic set in.

"I'm not going to kill you," he said. "But I will if you make a sound other than answering my questions when I remove the gag. Understand?"

She nodded.

He pulled the cloth down. She gasped for air and swallowed hard.

"Now listen carefully and answer me truthfully. If I find that you lied, I'll kill you."

"Why are you—"

"Shut up, Katrine." He pulled his pistol and aimed it at her head. She surprised him a bit when her face steeled instead of bursting into panic. "Was there someone else in Bruges? Was Noble working with someone else?"

"Th-there was this woman. Elizabeth, I think. She showed up at the restaurant after you killed those men." She looked down. "What's going on? Why are you doing this? Doesn't any of the past matter?"

"Oh, it matters. That's why Nev is dead." He shook his head as he slipped the gag back over her chin and set it in her mouth, then closed the trunk lid again. Before he was seated, his phone rang.

Dylan said, "I need you to cross check anyone with the name Elizabeth with Noble."

The guy said, "What?"

"I just received some fresh intel. He escaped Bruges with a woman named Elizabeth. I'm guessing there was some truth to the MI6 story. She might not be active now, but she was at some point. That should help narrow your search."

"OK, I'll get on that."

"Wait," Dylan said. "What did you find?"

"Went back and checked his primary contact's number. There were several failed calls and SMS messages to Noble's phone throughout the day. So, it wasn't them that cut off signal to his phone."

"Great to know. How's that help us?"

"It doesn't. But this does."

Dylan felt a film of sweat forming on his forehead while waiting for the man to continue. "Well, what?"

"Keep your pants on. I was verifying. Noble's contact received a call from the north part of Amsterdam only a few minutes ago."

"Can you get me a location?"

"Sending it now."

The phone buzzed in his hand. He swiped across the screen and tapped on the message app, then the link in the text. His map program pulled up. There were two dots. His location and the location of the phone.

"That's only a few minutes away." He hung up and peeled out of the alley toward the motorway.

CHAPTER 32

MY HANDS WERE TREMBLING. LEGS SHAKING. I STOOD IN front of the motel room door trying to suck down enough air to replenish the oxygen I'd lost from sprinting the half-mile back from the store. It felt as though the frigid wind turned the layer of sweat on my face into ice. The first drops of frozen rain pelted the ground, roof, and the few cars below.

After I somewhat caught my breath, I reached for the door. It cracked open before I grabbed the knob. The barrel of a pistol presented itself before the person carrying it. For a moment, I considered I was too late. But if that were the case, they wouldn't come to me. They'd wait until I entered.

"You OK?" Elizabeth asked. "You seem out of breath."

"Yeah. Hurried back here." I recapped my conversation with Clarissa.

"Did you get rid of the phones?" she asked.

I shook my head. "I have an idea." I led her to the bathroom, leaving the door open a crack to keep an eye on Lorraine.

"What's going on?"

"Someone tracked the phone Clarissa gave me. They have full control over it. She'd been calling and texting all day. She even tried to warn me before the shooting."

"So, they've seen all our movements today. That's how they got to the safe house."

"Yeah. There were times I had it turned off, or reception was poor. I think that's how we got the drop on the police station. I turned the phone off at the house." I paused a beat and pulled out the new phone. "I picked up a couple burner phones at the store, called her with one. Pretty certain that whoever had control of the phone she gave me will now start tracking this one."

"Why?"

"Because she's compromised. They have all her comms."

"OK, so what's your plan?"

"A little game of cat and mouse, and this phone is the cheese. But we don't have much time. Van de Berg has been close behind us. Now that there's two pings to track, I expect he'll show up sooner than later."

She nodded. "Are you going to kill him?"

"Eventually. First, we need to get info out of him, like where the hell is Katrine."

"You think he'll negotiate?"

"If Lorraine's relationship with him is what I think it is, he'll want to trade with us. Will that go down well? Your guess is as good as mine."

"We should get moving." She reached for the door.

"Wait." I blocked it with my arm. "Did you get anything out of her yet?"

"Refused to talk. I figured we'd have better luck with you here."

I bit down hard. Giving Lorraine up without gaining any intel was not ideal. They'd be in the wind with a chance to recoup and form a new plan to take me out. I'd deal with that later, though. "Most important thing right now is getting you two away from here."

"You don't think he's tracking her?"

"I think if that were the case, he'd have shown up immediately after we got her out of jail. Or he might've gotten to her first."

"Jack, do you think he took Katrine because she was there? Or—"

"There's gotta be some other reason." I glanced at my watch. We'd wasted too much time already. "All right, let's get moving."

Lorraine refused to get up. "There's no point. You'll never escape him, and when he finds us, he's likely to kill us. All of us, me included. I was told never to get caught, and if I did, don't bother showing up again." Her eyes misted over. "Doesn't matter what we do. He'll find us."

"Who does he work for?" I asked.

Lorraine shook her head. "Everybody and nobody."

"Strictly contract?" I asked.

She said nothing, stared straight ahead.

"Who feeds him intel?" Elizabeth asked. "I mean, I doubt it's you. Right? You're just a pretty face. I can imagine the type of jobs you work."

"Excuse me," Lorraine said. "I am plenty capable of gathering intel. He has an outside source, someone who…" She clenched her mouth shut. Her lips thinned into two white lines.

"That's a good start, Lorraine." I sat down on the bed across from her. "We don't know if he's aware we have you. But we know he has something that's important to us. I might be able to broker a trade."

She shook her head as those tears spilled over her eyelids. "He'll kill me."

"We'll take him down," Elizabeth said. "We both have the experience to do this. But we need your cooperation."

"How? What?" Lorraine wiped her face. Her cheeks reddened. Her fear turned to anger. "He's too good. Don't you realize that?"

We did, but what did that matter?

"You know him better than anybody," I said. "Will he be alone or will he have someone working with him?"

"Dylan trusts nobody," she said. "He won't even take me with him. We work together on the intel, but in the field, our contracts are our own."

"How do you know he didn't sell you out?" I said. "That he wasn't the one who alerted those men to your location?"

"He wouldn't," Lorraine said.

"Yeah? How much stuff did he have to lose in there?"

Lorraine sat with this for a minute, clearly stewing over the thought.

"You're confident there's no one he'd call in for backup?" Elizabeth asked.

"Yes." Lorraine swung her legs over the bed. "If he's on his way, we should go. I'll tell you more in the van."

Elizabeth looked up at me. I nodded.

"Get her down there and drive a little bit north."

"What about you?"

"I gotta get things set up in here. I'll find a place to monitor the situation and make a determination at that time."

"What kind of determination?"

I glanced at Lorraine and back at Elizabeth and shook my head. "Leave that up to me."

"OK, Jack. Be careful." She led Lorraine out to the van. A minute later, she exited the parking lot in the van with the lights off.

I set up the unused burner phone with a fresh SIM and called the other burner then tossed it on the bed. Then I tore a sheet of notebook paper out and scrawled a note for Van de Berg and placed it under the phone.

Frozen rain pelted the roof. The whomp-whomp of the heater fan rose and fell in a sputtering cycle. I switched off the main light. Left the bathroom light on and the door cracked. Enough light to indicate the room was occupied. Yet dim enough he'd be more cautious entering. I took one last look around. There was nothing left to do but wait.

CHAPTER 33

THE THUMPING AGAINST THE BACKSEAT INCREASED EVERY time Dylan slowed the vehicle to a stop. There had been several times he considered executing Katrine, ridding her from his life once and for all. It would be stupid, though. He realized that. Until he had Lorraine in hand, he'd have to let her live.

Then he'd dispose of her. There'd be no joy. And no remorse. There never was any of either when it came to killing.

Katrine had never been accepting of Dylan, despite being married to his cousin, Nev. She even spat at him on their wedding day. Maybe he'd deserved it. Was it wrong to try to sleep with her? He acknowledged most people would say yes, it was wrong.

But Dylan wasn't most people. Something was missing. That thing that most people had that told them what was right and wrong. Other people felt love and hate. And while, he'd sometimes feel anger, to him, everything was neutral. He existed in the moment and nothing else mattered.

He drove past the motel. The final ping had come from there. But moments prior, it had been a short distance down the road. He pulled up to the location. It appeared to be a market. There were some meth heads loitering out front. He drove a hundred meters further, turned around and drove back to the store. He pulled up next to the junkies.

"Seen anything unusual tonight?" Dylan asked them in Dutch.

No one looked his way.

"I said, have you seen anything unusual tonight?"

One of the women looked over at him. "Fuck off."

He smiled at her and said, "I hope you all will still be out here in ten minutes."

That was enough to break up the group. They split into pairs and got in different vehicles.

Dylan got a chuckle out of it, but as quickly as the humor in the situation had arisen, he put it to bed. There was a job to finish. One he'd been admonishing himself over for months. It wasn't often he failed. On the few occasions he had, he made up for it. He wasn't the best in the game for no reason, after all.

But Noble had been different. Dylan had lost him in Luxembourg, and shortly after that, the man vanished. Every single record gone. It was as if Jack Noble had never led the life that had led to Dylan being hired to terminate him.

All those months in between, they monitored his closest contacts. One by one, the ties severed. Until the day Clarissa Abbot surfaced in connection with Noble. He knew from that moment, it was only a matter of time before he had the man in his sights.

He had been correct about that.

He hadn't expected to screw it up again.

A couple cars occupied spaces in the motel parking lot. Dylan opted for an open spot near the stairs, the ones furthest from the office. That was by design. Before exiting the vehicle, he rethreaded the suppressor on his pistol and topped off the magazine. He didn't bother to holster it. There was no one around, and it would only require seconds he wouldn't have when he confronted Noble.

All but three rooms were pitch black. He considered two options. Enter all three, which would requiring the killing of three sets of people or harass whoever was working the office desk. Sticking to the wall on the main level, he hurried toward the office, keeping his pistol at his right side to hide it from the road.

The door jingled when he pushed it open. A middle-aged man with a stomach distended like a basketball was under his shirt leaned back in a chair smoking a cigarette. His white shirt was tight and transparent. His chest hair was visible and looked like a bunch of dead worms.

"Help you?" the guy said after blowing a plume of smoke overhead.

"Who's in each room?" Dylan demanded.

The guy narrowed his eyes as he looked Dylan over. Those eyes widened when he spotted the gun. He stammered as he tried to get up from his chair.

Dylan raised the pistol and aimed it at the man. He had no intention of killing him but would if it became necessary. "Just tell me who is in each room, and we won't have a problem."

"I-I-I can't remember."

"No. I won't accept that. Think. There's only three rooms occupied. This shouldn't be that hard."

"Right, right. Room 1 is always reserved for a couple of working girls. On the other end are two guys who've been with us for a couple weeks. Good guys. I don't think they want any trouble."

"And the third?"

"Just showed up today. Room 18. Here-here's a key." He twisted to the side and grabbed a key off a hook. That opens them all, but..." His voice trailed off as though he considered whether he should have said that.

"I just need the one room." He held out his hand and waited for the guy to throw it to him, caught it in mid-air when he did. "Now, what should I do with you?"

"Please, don't kill me."

Dylan shook his head and gestured toward the door behind the guy. "What's in there?"

"It's just a supply room."

"I want you to turn around and go to the door. Do not open it until I tell you to."

The guy choked on a sob but managed to compose himself quickly. "I've got kids."

"Good for you."

"Please don't kill me."

"If you say that again, I will. And I couldn't care less how that affects your kids. If you got a girl, it may lead to her working out of room 1 someday. So, do yourself, and her, a favor. Shut up and do what I say."

The man nodded as he leaned his forehead against the closed door. He held his hands at his side. He was hyperventilating. Would he pass out?

"OK," Dylan said after approaching the man. "Open the door."

The guy did. It was a storeroom, just as he'd said.

"Go to the corner and kneel down. Cross your legs at your ankles, lean your forehead against the wall, and place your hands behind your back." As the guy did as instructed, Dylan found a roll of zebra-print duct tape. "This is cute, you know. Do you do crafts with it?"

The guy looked back before putting his head against the wall. "It's my daughter's." His voice wavered now, and Dylan wondered whether he should just put a bullet in the weak man's brain. "I just want to give her a hug."

"All right, that's enough." Dylan tore off a long section of tape and wrapped it around the guy's wrists to secure him. Then he wrapped them with a larger section. The ankles followed. Finally, a strip across the mouth to keep the man from yelling. He pulled the guy off the wall and sat him down, then took a step back and admired his handiwork.

The guy's cheeks were red. His hair was soaked, as was his shirt. He stared at Dylan wide-eyed.

"I know this sucks. I'll make sure the police know soon enough." He turned and opened the door, stopped, and looked back. "But remember what I did for you here. I saved your life. Your daughter still has a father. Now, if, as a father, you want to keep your daughter alive, you'll tell the police nothing about me. Understand?"

The man tried to speak through the tape but realized it was pointless. He started nodding and his eyes clenched shut and the tears started flowing.

Dylan reached back as he exited the supply room and cut the lights before shutting the door. In the office, he turned off the computer monitor and dimmed the overhead lights. It would look closed from the street, not that anyone would be stopping. But he didn't need some prostitute poking her nose in asking for clean sheets. As he left, he flipped the open sign to closed.

The weather had gotten worse in the time he'd been in the office. The frozen rain pelted him sideways as he stepped outside. Perhaps after this he'd finally relocate to Portugal. Live by the sea in a small fishing village. Cut off access to everyone in the world. That would be the life. For the first time ever, free from carrying out the wishes of sick bastards. From his father to the president of Paraguay, he'd worked for them all. And he'd kill them all for enough money.

Some he might eliminate for free.

He hustled up the first set of stairs and walked to the other end of the building. The only room occupied on this level was Noble's. Stopping short of the window, he paused long enough to paint a picture of what was going on in the room. It turned out to be not much. It was quiet. Perhaps they were all sleeping. That would make the task that much easier. Not only would he have the element of surprise, his victims would have no idea he'd ever been there.

Dylan retrieved the key from his pocket and slid it into the lock, twisting it and the knob at the same time. The door eased open. For as dilapidated as the motel looked, they kept the hinges well oiled. And for that, he was appreciative.

The empty room with perfectly made beds, however, pissed him off.

"Bastards," he muttered. He was about to check the bathroom when he stopped to investigate the phone on the bed. It was sitting atop a piece of paper that had one word written on it: SMILE. Upon closer examination, he saw the phone was connected, the call timer counting up, now at seven minutes.

He put the phone to his ear. "Hello?"

CHAPTER 34

JACK SHELTERED IN AN EMPTY OFFICE ACROSS THE STREET
from the motel, shielded from the wind and rain, the latter of which
impaired his visibility. Still, he managed to make out Dylan Van de Berg as
he exited his car, went to the office, and then climbed the stairs to the
room a few minutes later. The wait felt like hours, even though it took less
than three minutes from the time he pulled in to when he entered the
room. A few seconds after that, he heard Van de Berg's voice on the line.

Jack waited a few beats before replying. "I hear you've been looking
for me."

The sharp intake of air was followed by a long exhale. "Jack Noble, I
presume."

"Dylan Van de Berg, I surmise."

"I see Lorraine can't be trusted the way I thought she could."

I watched as he parted the blinds a few inches and scanned the parking
lot.

"No," I said. "She's been pretty steadfast, refusing to talk to us. We
knew your name before finding her. MI6 has been onto you for a while."

"Bullshit." The blinds fell shut. "No matter to me what happens to her.
You know the reason Schreiber died instead of you was due to her poor
planning."

Was he bluffing? Trying to make me think he'd let the woman die if it came to it? I decided not to play his game. "You. Her. It doesn't matter to me who pulled the trigger. You were the one in Bruges. We already know that."

"Where are you now, Noble? We can settle this like men, if you're up to it."

"I've got no beef with you," I said. "What I want is to know who's behind this. Who's paying you to kill me?"

Van de Berg laughed. "You don't want to know that, Noble. And, to tell you the truth, I'm doing this more for myself than I am them at this point. I told them to keep the money. I don't want it. I just want to see you die."

"Pretty pathetic if that's your life goal. What are you gonna do after I'm gone? Everything'll be boring when you go back to killing unknowing citizens."

"I think I'll figure it out. Perhaps I'll start a crusade. Clarissa Abbot would make a nice trophy. And then there's Bear, Riley Logan. And isn't there a child he's adopted?"

I let the air hang between us and didn't respond.

"But that's not the only kid, right, Jack? Little Mia…and don't forget your brother and his family. They wouldn't stand a chance against me."

"I wouldn't underestimate any of them, including my brother. He used to kick my ass all the time when we were kids. He'd get the better of you."

Dylan chuckled again, but his tone became much more serious. "This will end soon, Noble, with one of us dead on the ground."

"I go, Lorraine goes, too."

"If I go, your new girlfriend Katrine goes, too."

"Why don't you tell me where she is. We can just end this now."

"Good luck with that. Something happens to me, she dies."

Finally, we'd reached the point in the conversation I'd been waiting for. "I don't believe for a minute Lorraine means nothing to you. Yeah, I get that you're a narcissistic psychopath and all that shit. But you've kept her close for years now. Hell, from what we gather, you were lingering in courtrooms looking for your next apprentice when you found her. Could've picked anyone from a number of branches of the military or within a number of agencies. Yet, you took a cute blonde who'd never been given a chance, and you turned her into your protégé."

Dylan was silent.

"Got to the point where you divvied the work, took on more jobs, let her plan her own ops. I know it wasn't her in Luxembourg City. You know how?"

He remained silent.

"She wouldn't have missed me."

"Maybe I didn't miss you. You ever think about that? I could've been there for Schreiber."

He was buying time at this point. Probably had someone trying to figure out where my call was coming from.

"Red Light District. The bridge south of The Oude Church. Stand on the east side with Katrine. No one else. I'll have Lorraine with me. You'll send Katrine to the middle of the bridge. Then I'll release Lorraine. You've got one hour. If you're not there, Lorraine dies."

I ended the call before he could reply. Didn't need to hear his words to gauge his reaction. The chair busting through the window told me all I needed to know. He hustled through the door, leaving it wide open. Had a cell phone in his hand. Maybe mine. Hopefully mine. I knew the one I had was worthless now, so I pulled the SIM, snapped it, and discarded it and the phone in a gutter.

Van de Berg peeled out of the parking lot and sped down the road. Would he be on the bridge? Would he have someone else in place on my end? Over the years, the guy had built up a network of connections. How loyal were they to him? That's the problem with transactional relationships. Once the transaction has been completed, there's no relationship. All you had to do was look around some of the seedier areas of the Red Light District to see that.

I stood a few feet off the road and waited for Elizabeth to pull the van to the curb.

"How'd it go?"

I told her where the exchange would go down. From the backseat, Lorraine sighed, relieved that Van de Berg cared enough to make the trade. Now that she was compromised, I gave it a fifty percent chance he'd pullet a bullet in the back of her head the first opportunity he got.

Lorraine's presence made it difficult for Elizabeth and me to strategize.

I had no problem making a clean exchange. But what if it went awry? We both knew the guy couldn't be trusted. Once he gave up Katrine, he'd have to start all over with me. It wouldn't be as easy this time with the knowledge of how he'd compromised my network. In time, we'd figure out who was working against me. They'd lead us to Van de Berg.

Elizabeth parked in an empty lot so we could talk. We stood in the wind and rain and went over the details. The plan was set.

CHAPTER 35

THE RAIN GAVE WAY TO CLEARING SKIES. THE WIND GUSTS died down and were almost nonexistent further in the city, where clusters of buildings lined the streets. I walked along the canal, in front of the church. Its steeples adorned with crosses rose into the sky in stark contrast to the reason we were there.

Lorraine walked by my side, hand-in-hand. She was no longer in restraints. She said she'd cooperate, but without fully understanding her relationship with Van de Berg, I feared she'd run. The only way forward was to maintain contact. Once the time came to make the exchange, she'd have no path but forward toward Dylan.

We had no time to secure a decent comms system, so the two cell phones we picked up on the way into town combined with earbuds would have to do.

"I'm all set," Elizabeth said. "I can see you two."

I glanced across the canal and scanned the street for her.

"See me?" she asked.

"No."

"Good. He won't either, but I'll have eyes on him the whole time."

"Where the hell are you?"

"See the lady of the night standing in front of the brothel directly across from you?"

I glanced across the canal. "Not too shabby, Lizzy. All right, speaking of time, we're down to a few minutes left. I'm gonna linger back here. You spot him, let me know."

"Roger that."

We muted our phones and the line fell silent. The hum of the crowd spilled into the night like oil over water, hovering just above, never mingling. The broad range of the types of people I saw was fascinating. Families from Iowa. Sailors on leave looking for some action. Degenerates here and there, mostly keeping to themselves. What else could they do? This was a high visibility location, even without tourists. That's why we chose it.

"I'm not sure I want to go back to him," Lorraine said.

I glanced at her. "What?"

"I have this feeling." She pulled us to a stop and looked across the canal. "He's going to kill me."

"Kill him first. That's what I'd do."

She shook her head. "What if I tell you everything? All his hideouts, the people he works for, how he plans his missions. All of it. I can do that. Let me do that."

"One, you had your chance, and you clammed up. Two, he's got someone who's grown on me far more than you have. As far as I'm concerned, one less spy roaming the streets is a good thing. Two less would be even better. You can kill each other, for all I care."

We took a few more steps before she stopped again, like a toddler about to throw a tantrum. "What if I scream?"

"You wouldn't."

"Oh yeah?" She pulled back a foot or so and opened her mouth.

I yanked her toward me. We were chest-to-chest, mouth-to-mouth. I wrapped one arm around her back. The other pulled the pistol in my coat pocket and pressed it into her stomach. I pulled back from the kiss but kept our bodies tight.

"Do you know me?" I questioned. "Who I am? What I'm capable of? You've been partnered with a man who's been trying to kill me for a year. You think your life means anything to me?"

Tears spilled down her cheeks. At that moment, I realized she truly feared what Van de Berg would do when he had her in his possession.

I unmuted my phone and said, "Change of plans."

"What?" Elizabeth said. "Jack, this isn't—"

"You follow them after the exchange. Stay back. Don't get involved. Once I get Katrine safe, we'll take Van de Berg down."

"You know it won't be that easy."

"Right, chances are he'll get off the main road after a block or two where he'll have some sort of transportation waiting. At that point, stop them."

"What the bloody hell are you talking about, Jack?"

"Yeah, yeah, just like that. Keep our comms open, and I'll have your back inside thirty seconds." I paused a beat, waiting to see if Elizabeth still needed clarification. She said nothing. I figured she understood this was all to pump Lorraine up enough to go through with this. "So, we're good?"

"Yeah, I think I got you."

"Going dark again." I pretended to mute the line and let Lorraine step back. "Good?"

She bobbed her head up and down an inch. "Yes, but I'm still scared. Can you give me a gun?"

I got a laugh out of that. "On a basic human level, I have some empathy for you. But I'm not fucking stupid, lady. Last person I'm giving a weapon to is a trained assassin who wants me dead."

She huffed and started walking again. The whole thing had been a show.

"She must be quite the actress," Elizabeth said.

I glanced across the canal and gave a quick nod.

"She's a damn psychopath, Jack. Don't forget that." A few beats passed. "I see him. He's here. He's got Katrine with him. I can take him out here."

I turned my head and whispered, "No, you'll be seen and booked for murder."

We took a few more steps before I looked toward the other side of the bridge. A couple groups of people passed each other going opposite directions. As they dispersed, I saw Katrine scanning the area ahead of her, a look of desperation on her face. Aside from that, she appeared OK, though mentally I was sure she had been scarred.

Van de Berg stood next to her. His coat came to mid-thigh. Long enough to conceal a short rifle or shotgun.

"Be ready to take him out," I said to Elizabeth. "Don't like that jacket. Might have something under there."

Lorraine gasped, no doubt out of concern for her partner. I shot her a look, and she glanced at the ground.

"I'm ready," Elizabeth whispered.

"How close are you?"

She didn't reply. I had to take a harder look and make sure no one else was present. For the most part, the crowds went about their business, oblivious to the situation playing out in front of them. But, then again, wasn't that always the way? We don't always operate in the shadows, and the world has no idea.

Van de Berg locked eyes with me when we reached the bridge entrance. I nodded once. He did the same. It was odd being face to face with the guy who had been hunting me for some time. But I brushed that aside.

The exchange was going down now.

I hoped like hell we all survived it.

CHAPTER 36

IT WAS A SCENE OUT OF A WESTERN. I STOOD AT ONE END OF the bridge, my jacket unzipped, pistol easy to access, a woman at my side. Van de Berg had unbuttoned his coat, too. A gust of wind opened it a bit, confirmed my fear that he was hiding a weapon under there. A short shotgun. He wasn't going to hit me with that from across the bridge. The accuracy wasn't there. It was an ambush weapon, good for crowd control. Whether he was doing the ambushing or getting ambushed was the question. Either way, I was certain he had something else on him.

Katrine broke into tears. Van de Berg grabbed her arm and kept her upright until she composed herself. He said something to her. She nodded and wiped the tears from her eyes and took a deep breath. A group of pedestrians pushed past them and gathered in the middle of the bridge for photographs.

"He still there?" I asked Elizabeth.

"I've got him," she said.

"OK. Keep your distance. We can't have him turn around and spot you. He'll pull that shotgun and send six rounds of buckshot your way."

The crowd continued on, smiling and laughing and talking. I gripped Lorraine's arm tighter as they passed us. She remained quiet, still. I wondered what was going through her mind.

Now the bridge was empty. The crowds on the streets along the canal had thinned. There wouldn't be another opportunity like this.

"Take ten steps and stop," I said to Lorraine. "Don't move until you see Katrine walking toward us. I want you both to hit the middle of the bridge at the same time. Understand?"

She stared ahead, said nothing.

"Lorraine, do you hear me?"

She nodded, glanced at me. "I'm ready." With that, she took ten steps and stopped.

On the other side, Van de Berg kept his eyes on me, leaned his head toward Katrine, and told her to go.

The women both walked slowly down the middle of the bridge. Lorraine mirrored Katrine's movements as she moved toward the railing.

"I don't like this," I said.

"Me either," Elizabeth said. "What's she going to do? Push her?"

Had there been some signal between Lorraine and Van de Berg I had missed? Could the two of them have planned for this specific scenario?

"Get ready for—"

"Shit, Jack." Van de Berg had just dropped his coat. "He's got a rifle strapped to his back." She left her position and was now exposed.

"Get back under cover." I couldn't keep my focus on all four of them.

And that's when it went all to shit.

Elizabeth grunted, said, "Get the hell off me."

I took my focus off Katrine and Lorraine and searched for Elizabeth. I saw some men near her previous position, couldn't see past them. The light overhead blinked orange and yellow and white.

"Someone's got me, Jack. Watch—"

The line went dead. I shifted my eyes to the right, saw Van de Berg reaching one arm over his head, behind his back. A moment later, he produced a small rifle. A woman screamed. He chambered a round. Behind him, a man hoisted Elizabeth in the air, trying to get her over his shoulder. She gauged his face and stuck her thumbs in his eyes.

The first shot rang out as I drew my pistol and dashed to the left to take cover behind the concrete pillar at the base of the bridge.

Katrine's eyes went wide. Her coat fell open. A red spot bloomed on her chest.

I fired a round into the water. Van de Berg was too far for me to get a clean shot from this distance with a 9mm. Elizabeth had to take him out. I shouted as much into the mic, hoping she could still hear me.

Van de Berg chambered another round. Lorraine froze. He was locked in on her. But he hesitated. Understandable, given their relationship, but unacceptable, given his experience.

Lorraine glanced left, then right. In a fluid motion, she lunged toward the side of the bridge, placed a hand on the railing, and vaulted over it, going in the water feet first at the same moment the crack of Dylan firing the rifle roared above the chaos.

My first instinct was to jump into the frigid water and rescue her. I held back. There was no point in risking my life for her.

I heard another gunshot, looked across the canal, saw a man staggering backward into the street. An oncoming vehicle plowed into him, sent him flying twenty feet in the air. He hit the ground and rolled down the bank into the water.

Elizabeth emerged from the group of guys that had harassed her and swept the scene with her pistol. I was scanning the road as well. We settled on each other, shaking our heads.

Van de Berg had fled.

"Jack! Jack!" Elizabeth's voice came across loud though the earpiece.

"I'm here. You see him?"

"No."

"I gotta get to Katrine."

"He'll pick you off, Jack. Plus, the cops will be here any moment. You can't be caught on that bridge."

Sirens rose in the distance. I looked for the strobes reflecting off the buildings, but there were so many lights in the area, I'd never see the police cars before they were on the street.

"They'll attend to her," Elizabeth said.

"He's probably left. I'm gonna check on her."

"Jack, come on, the cops will arrest you. You'll be a sitting duck in jail. You know this. You gotta leave her."

I looked down the bridge and knew it wouldn't matter. Katrine was on her back, head to the side. Her shirt was completely red. She was gone. All I could think of was Bernie, how she'd react. And how Mia might act if the situation ended with me dead on the ground.

I tucked my pistol away and found the shadows. "Meet me at the Hotel MAI, like we planned."

CHAPTER 37

DYLAN DIDN'T STOP RUNNING UNTIL THE SIRENS FADED INTO a song whistling above the hum of the city. His heart pounded, blood whooshed in his ears, and his side cramped. The side effect of letting his conditioning drop too low. Still, he had just sprinted farther than most men could. Someone could do better, though, and that meant he wasn't good enough.

He had ditched the rifle, throwing it into the canal when he reached the other side of the bridge entrance. The shotgun was unfortunately still on the bridge along with his coat. At least he had his pistol, not that it would do him any good from a distance.

The sweat coating his body amplified the chill in the air, but that didn't bother him. He kept moving to avoid looking suspicious and to survey the canal. The current traveled the same way he had. He stayed close to the canal, looking for signs of Lorraine. So far, there'd been nothing. Not even her jacket.

They both practiced the Wim Hof method. Known better as the Iceman, Hof was famous for his breathing method that gave him an insane tolerance to cold and the ability to hold his breath for superhuman periods of time. At their peak of training, Lorraine had bested Dylan by more than ninety seconds. She wasn't as strong as she used to be, but the woman could still spend three minutes or so in the icy water without coming up for air.

He reached down and scooped up a handful of loose rock, which he tossed into the water. He recalled those few moments where he stared Lorraine down and admonished himself for not taking the shot sooner. What had happened there? How had he been so reckless? Her time had come to an end. He had no more use for her. And she knew he was about to shoot her. Why else would she jump?

If she had survived the plunge, he'd face his biggest risk ever during his time in this business. She knew him like no other. How he thought. Where he'd go next. How long he'd hide out. He had to break the pattern. Do something she would never expect.

He reached into his pocket for the phone Noble had left in the motel room. There were no calls, no messages. Yet. Noble would reach out, he was sure of it.

Dylan stopped and looked back at the scene on the bridge. There were police everywhere. Their strobes merged with the city lights and faded into the heavens.

There was no doubt he'd been caught on camera. That's why he agreed and even didn't mind the location. Sure, his face would be all over the news, but so would Noble's. And that meant Jack would have an impossible time going underground again. The coverage would flush him out, cause him to make a poor decision, like trying to end it with Dylan, who would now have the advantage.

"Just need to wait it out." He slid the phone back in his pocket and continued on, keeping an eye on the canal.

He passed the local university and recalled that the canal emptied into another soon. The perfect place for Lorraine to exit. He hurried down the road and across the bridge on Grimburwal and stopped at the steps leading up from the water.

His stomach knotted, his mouth went dry. Lorraine's coat was draped over a couple of the steps. He backpedaled to the nearest wall and scanned the area left to right and back again.

His plan meant he couldn't miss, yet he did. Even so, her only escape was into the icy waters, which she had taken. He had hoped, given the conditions, she wouldn't make it out of the water alive.

But she had.

She couldn't remain on the loose.

The fear left, replaced by a new determination to find her. Where had she gone? Where would he go? If there was one consolation, he told himself, she was in no condition to fight him now. She needed to get out of those clothes. Get warm.

Definitely not the way he had just come. He continued on his path, past the canals. He reached a tourist shop, souvenirs and shit like that. Across the street was a ladies' clothing store. He dodged an oncoming vehicle and entered through the front door, which dinged as he stepped through. A woman greeted him. Her eyes betrayed her smile. She backed off when he shot her a look.

There were a half-dozen shoppers present. All glanced in his direction. All broke off eye contact almost immediately.

Lorraine was here. It was all but confirmed when his foot slipped a few inches on a puddle. He looked back at the associate. She was on the phone, her gaze on the dressing rooms.

Dylan retrieved his pistol. Didn't bother with the suppressor. He'd shoot everyone left in the store after he took care of Lorraine.

A woman attempted to block his path to the back of the store where the dressing rooms were located. She posted up, held out her hand, told him, "Stop."

He chuckled at her, raised the pistol and aimed it at her face. "Get the fuck out of my way."

Her eyes grew wide as she realized this wasn't some guy merely chasing a woman. "Don't shoot."

Using his free hand, he shoved her into a rack of dresses and continued past the saloon style doors separating the shop from the back. There were four louvered doors, two per side. One was cracked open. He pushed it with the pistol barrel and confirmed it was empty.

Lorraine had to be unarmed. There was no way Noble would hand her a pistol or a knife or anything like that. Unless she had sold Dylan out.

That was the problem here. He had no idea what she had told Noble and the woman.

"Lorraine," he said. "Why not come out and talk? I just need to know what you said to them. We can talk here, no problem."

Of course, he had no intention of talking to her again. And staying here? The lady who greeted him was no doubt on the phone with the police. Given their presence at the bridge, it would only take a couple of minutes for an officer to arrive.

He opened the second door. Empty. Then the third. Nothing.

Easing past the fourth door, he reached for the knob and turned it then forced the door open quickly. At the same time, he whipped himself around, squaring up with the opening, pistol aimed straight ahead.

But there was no one to shoot.

However, Lorraine's wet clothes were on the ground in a pile.

"Dammit."

The ding of the door broke his focus. He heard a man's voice. The woman replied in a hushed tone. Dylan headed for the backdoor, which opened outward. The cold rushed in. He slammed it, grabbed a pallet on the ground and jammed the door shut with it. It wouldn't buy him much time. But it would be enough.

He sprinted to the left until the alley opened up to a busy road where he was able to integrate into a mob of people following a tour guide.

A few blocks later, he found his offramp and disappeared into the night.

CHAPTER 38

THREE DAYS HAD PASSED SINCE THE DISASTER IN AMSTERDAM. The image of Katrine bleeding out on the bridge remained fresh, played on repeat in the movie theater of my mind.

Though Elizabeth begged me not to leave, I traveled to Bruges to Katrine's sister-in-law's house and delivered the news to her and Bernie. It had to be done in person. And I had to do it, no matter how difficult it would be to look that little girl in the eye and tell her that her mother had died. She was mixed up in this thing because of me. Or so I had thought. The woman explained a few things to me about Van de Berg and her brother, Nev. The men were cousins.

Most of the family had shunned Van de Berg, but Nev had remained in communication, and was ultimately played by his cousin. Despite the bad blood that had developed between the men, Nev agreed to help in Barcelona. Dylan killed him and left him in the building, expecting to be able to fake his own death.

There was no way to prove what Nev's sister had said, but she believed it. Was Van de Berg really trying to fake his own death? Was he getting rid of his cousin over a dispute—the bad blood in the family she had mentioned—or had something happened in Barcelona that finally severed the relationship?

I wanted the answers to those questions. The evidence we had pointed to something different. A relationship gone sour over splitting the money. Maybe Nev had spoken out of turn to someone. Maybe Van de Berg's psychopathic tendencies won out and he executed his cousin, thinking DNA would match close enough to rule him as dead once he went off the grid.

I wanted Van de Berg dead more, though.

With every passing hour, chances we'd find him grew slimmer. He could be anywhere in Europe. Like me, he had exit plans in place if they were needed. Numbered accounts. Other vessels to store money. Fake identities. Safehouses. Everything a growing boy needs.

Following my brief trip to Bruges, Elizabeth and I holed up an hour south of Amsterdam, on the border with Belgium. She had a contact who let us use their guesthouse. We bought a few laptops and some other equipment and monitored the cell phone I left in the hotel room.

It had been offline until two minutes ago.

"I've almost got it." Elizabeth leaned in close to the screen. "Yes, yes, almost...there, got it!"

I squeezed in next to her, and together we huddled over the thirteen-inch laptop screen. "He's outside Amsterdam."

Elizabeth glanced at me. "You think Lorraine survived?"

That had been another question. The woman jumped over the bridge and, as far as we knew, hadn't resurfaced. Dive teams had worked the canal for thirty-six hours following the incident and come up empty-handed. We heard her jacket was found, but nothing more.

"It would explain why he hung around. At the same time, it doesn't. He was going to kill her. He could've shot at me. Instead, he chose her."

"Do you think they planned it that way?" Elizabeth tapped on the keyboard to zoom in on the pin. "Could they have thought through every situation, and if that specific one were to occur, would they have planned for her to jump?"

"Sounds pretty stupid when you put it that way." I recalled the scene for the hundredth time. Van de Berg looked me dead in the eye after shooting Katrine. Then he aimed at Lorraine. She jumped. "It makes more sense that he was aiming to kill. After shooting Katrine, any chance of a clean escape for the two of them was out. He figured she talked to us, gave up some secrets. Perhaps he thought she agreed to work with us."

"Couldn't have been the best relationship."

"Think about any relationship you've had with another spook. How'd it go?"

"Not well."

"Exactly. We're all too damn paranoid. He pegged her as rolling over and cooperating."

"So, she survived, and he's hanging around looking for her." Elizabeth's brow furrowed, and she began tapping at the keyboard again. "We're losing it."

"Screenshot it, at least we'll have the general area. Once we get there, we can determine how strong the signal is. That'll give us our radius to work from."

A while later, we came to a stop on a street corner in the southern outskirts of Amsterdam. We decided to work from the inside out. Took up position across the street from the location of the phone. The actual phone might've been within three meters of the location. Or it could've been a mile. All depended on the strength of signal at that moment. Looking at the cell phones we'd brought with us, the signal was strong here. We just had to hope.

There were no public options for us here. No hotels or stores that had good visibility. So we parked on the street a block down and stared at the building, a three story apartment building with a coffee shop and offices on the first level. The foot traffic on the street was steady. Vehicle traffic minimal.

"Think he's up there?" Elizabeth asked.

"I think the phone is. I think he was there at one point. Now, I'm not so sure. He could've deliberately turned it on to draw us out. Which is fine by me. I want to end this now. Today."

"Me as well. I'm gonna go get some coffee. Want one?"

"Yeah. Make it two. Extra strength."

"OK. Keep your phone handy. Going to circle the block and see if anything stands out."

I watched her in the rearview as she hurried down the street, coat collar pulled up with her hair tucked in it. Splitting up like this, even for a few minutes, wasn't ideal even if it could be beneficial.

I placed myself in Van de Berg's shoes. Would I stay this close to the scene? If so, why? It all came back to Lorraine. But was I over- or underthinking it? The phone turned on long enough for us to establish a location. Then the signal died.

Thinking through the possible scenarios of why he powered the phone on, I landed on this. Van de Berg figured we had planted the other phone —the one I used to speak with him—on Lorraine. Why would he think this? Because we'd then track them with the phone.

His reasoning for turning it on was to see if she had reached out to him. He didn't consider we were monitoring. Or he did, and just didn't care. Hell, he might be in the same place as me.

Let's finish this.

I took a look in the mirror again. Elizabeth was gone. I redirected my focus to the building, watched a nine-by-nine section of windows. Nothing happened. For the next fifteen minutes, I shifted my gaze all around, capturing every face that walked past and running them through an internal memory bank for matches. There were none.

Elizabeth turned the corner ahead and walked in front of the target building. She slowed by the entrance, turned, looked inside. Her expression remained the same when she looked over in my direction. Seemed that way, at least. The large sunglasses hid a portion of her face.

She ducked into the coffee shop, and I lost sight of her. I shifted my gaze to the end of the building where she had turned from and looked for anyone that might be a tail. Anyone out of place. No one fit the bill.

I started to think we were in the wrong place.

The people running out of the coffee shop told me how wrong I was.

CHAPTER 39

"HE'S GOT A GUN!"

The woman clutching her infant to her chest ran into a couple of pedestrians as she hurried away from the cafe, terror written across her face. Everyone on the street froze in place as more people rushed out of the building.

Everyone but Elizabeth.

I jumped out of the car, pulled my pistol out, and ran to the other side of the street. There was shouting and screaming and even sobbing. Had someone been shot? I hadn't heard gunfire but that meant nothing. Van de Berg could've used a suppressor. It wouldn't totally silence his weapon, but from where I was, I'd have never heard it.

I blocked someone hurrying away. "What's going on?"

"There's a man in there with a gun. He shot some woman." The lady forced her way past me.

I fought back the panic that threatened to overtake my body. Didn't matter how many times I'd been in these situations, it was always there in the background, threatening to overtake me. It was a good thing, though. Kept me sharp and on top of things.

I wasn't going to solve the problem on the street. There was no way to tell what was happening inside, though I could picture it. He got the drop on Elizabeth and probably fled.

The door whipped open as a young couple fled. I stepped into it before it fell shut. The scene unfolded. A young barista frozen at the counter, eyes wide, mouth open. Others were down on the ground. A few patrons hid under their tables. The rest of what I saw didn't match the scene in my head.

To my right, a man was attending to someone on the ground, applying pressure to an abdominal gunshot wound. I was expecting Elizabeth. It wasn't her.

"Lorraine?" I dropped to a knee beside her. "Lorraine, can you hear me?"

Her eyes fluttered open. She nodded. "He got the drop on me." Her face was growing paler by the second. A trickle of blood escaped her lips. "I thought I had him this time."

"Elizabeth?"

Lorraine stuttered but couldn't manage any more words. She lifted her arm a little, pointed toward the back.

"Does he have her?"

The guy aiding her spoke up. "The other lady went after him."

"Through the back," the woman next to him said.

I followed her extended finger to the hallway on the left side of the back wall. Before leaving, I placed my hand over Lorraine's. "Hang in there. Help is on the way."

She gripped my fingers in her palm. "K-k-kill...him."

"Oh God," the man said. "I think she's crashing."

Lorraine's grip loosened as her eyes fell shut.

"CPR," I said. "Don't stop until the medics get here." With that, I dashed to the back of the cafe and through the swinging door leading to the kitchen.

A man hiding behind a stainless-steel table pointed at the back door. "Through there."

I put my shoulder into the door. It whipped open. My eyes adjusted to the sun. I saw Van de Berg sprinting toward an ally.

"Jack."

I looked over and saw Elizabeth slumped against the wall. "Not you, too."

She pulled her hand away from her chest, revealing the gunshot wound. I pulled the door open and yelled inside.

"Make sure the medics know there's a woman down out here. Got it?" I waited a beat. "You hear me?"

The guy popped his head up and nodded.

"Get out there and tell them! Then get back here and help her." I turned back to Elizabeth. "I can't let him get away."

"Go, Jack." She tried to smile. "I'm going to be OK. It just hurts like a bitch."

I took one last look at her and then sprinted in the direction of Van de Berg. I reached the alley. He'd already made it to another intersection and was turning right. I pushed forward, sprinting harder than before. I reached the corner, took the turn tight. Saw Van de Berg at the last second step out from the alcove and attempt to body check me. I had just enough time to angle my body to lead with my shoulder, as though he were a linebacker standing in my way of the goal line.

We collided hard.

My shoulder screamed in pain, dislocated, rendering my right arm useless. I flew a good eight feet and came down on the sidewalk hard. The rough surface grated against my face, neck, arms. I rolled through the fall and came to rest on my knee. I looked back. Van de Berg was on his stomach, trying to get to his hands and knees. His pistol had skidded a good ten feet away. I'd lost mine in the fall.

"Van de Berg!"

He forced himself forward like a sea lion on wet sand. I managed to get to my feet and stagger toward him, shaking off the cobwebs with each step. He was almost to his gun and would make it before me, so I dove on top of him, making sure I hit the back of his head with my forearm. Now my left arm screamed out in pain. I rolled forward a bit, which did some good. My right shoulder popped back into place. The arm still didn't move well, but I had some functionality back.

Van de Berg squirmed under me, rolled onto his side. He swung hard at my head. The first blow got me, but I dodged the second and threaded my arm under his. He grabbed the back of my hair and pulled hard. I brought my hand up and over the back of his shoulder, then wrapped it inward until my palm was on his neck. I pushed it back as hard as I could, gripping his Adam's Apple, while moving my right hand around the back of his head, pulling it toward me. He was trying to do the same to me but couldn't secure his other hand on my throat.

I was like a pit bull. Someone would have to shoot me to get me to stop before the man was dead.

Van de Berg's eyes were wide, looked like they were gonna pop out. His face turned a dark shade of purple. His tongue protruded from his mouth. He'd be dead inside a minute.

Not good enough.

I pushed with one hand and pulled with the other, using as much opposing force as I could muster and snapped his neck. He let go of my hair. His body went limp. I pushed off of him and rolled onto my back. The sun was overhead, shone with full force down on the narrow alley.

Sitting up, I looked for witnesses. The alley was deserted. There were no balconies on the buildings on either side. Few windows.

I checked Van de Berg for a pulse and confirmed what I already knew.

He was dead.

Only one thing left to do with him. Hide the body. A dumpster did the trick until we could get a cleanup crew out here to get rid of him for good.

CHAPTER 40

"They say I'll make a full recovery." Elizabeth grinned from the other side of the phone on a video chat. It had been too risky for me to visit her in the hospital. Even with her connections, she couldn't get me past the guards to her room. It had taken a couple of surgeries, but she pulled through and wouldn't have lasting issues. The short term was gonna be rough, but she was a tough woman. I had no doubt she'd make it.

"We'll have to meet for a beer or something once you're out," I said. "Any idea when that'll be?"

"They said a few days. Lots of rehab ahead, of course. Probably return to London for a bit for that."

"Gonna stick around there?"

"Maybe. I heard there's an opening at MI6 if I want it."

"I could certainly use a good contact there again."

She laughed. "No, Jack, what you need to do is get back to that little girl and give her the life she deserves."

I looked away from the screen. "I've come to realize she already has it. Sean's a better dad than I'll ever be, and she's already spent most of the past couple of years with him. Maybe it's best for her if I don't disrupt that."

Elizabeth nodded, though she looked sad. "You'll do what's right. I know you will."

"Any news on Lorraine?"

Elizabeth's lips thinned, turned white. She shook her head, looked down. "Lorraine didn't make it. Sad story, there."

"Yeah, unfortunate. I don't know how she would've handled the world after all that, though."

"The same way as you and me, Jack."

"I disagree. We started off on the right path. Sure, I deviated, but I came back. I don't think Lorraine ever had a chance. Something was always off." I paused a beat. "To the best of your knowledge, the other thing is taken care of?"

Elizabeth nodded once, said nothing. There was no need. Dylan Van de Berg's name never needed to be spoken again.

"Guess I should get going," I said.

"Will you contact me again?" Elizabeth asked.

"I told you we'd meet for beers."

She looked sad. "For some reason, I don't believe you."

"This may be finished, but I still have work to do. Clarissa needs my help. I intend to give it to her."

"If you ever need a hand, with anything at all, you reach out, Jack."

We said goodbye and hung up.

Next, I called the dial-in Clarissa gave me. All I got was a fast busy, indicating it had been disabled. That wasn't a comforting feeling. Maybe she and Beck would show up later. They did it once, they could do it again.

Finally, I called the French number I'd found in the hotel room. This time someone answered.

"DSGE, Agent DuPont."

I hung up, dismantled the phone and tossed it in the trash behind the bar. DSGE. I thought back to my old associate Peirre. I wondered if he had known this DuPont before he died. I'd ask the agent when I showed up at his house.

Before leaving, I drained my beer and left the bartender a fifty to say he never saw me. Outside the small pub, I flagged down a taxi, had him drive me two miles down the road and drop me off at a rental I'd found online.

Once inside, I slid the bag off my shoulder and retrieved the laptop.

Van de Berg's laptop.

A day after the final incident, I found the room the phone had pinged from. There wasn't much there. Just the laptop and some notebooks and a digital card that, when accessed, displayed one hell of a balance. From the notebooks, I was able to determine the pin to the computer. I guess the guy never figured the device would be confiscated. Or maybe Lorraine had been the one to write the instructions in the back of the black notebook for a situation such as this. If so, she'd won.

After searching through and using the encryption pin found in the notebook, I was sitting on the keys to six wallets that I assumed correlated to six of the ten addresses displayed on the device.

I had his login to the job board, too. Pulling it open again, I was greeted with something other than a blank pea-green screen. This time, there was a message waiting. Below it a prompt. I typed in exactly what was written on the page, and a new message appeared.

"Glad to see you are back. Thought you might've eaten a bullet."

I took a moment before replying. "Still going strong. Lorraine not so much, but it was me or her. She turned."

"Not good. How do I know you're not going the same direction?"

"Give me another job. You'll see."

"It's incoming already. This one is sure to bring Noble to your doorstep." The cursor blinked for what felt like an eternity. "Update me soon."

I sat back and waited for what would come next. Five minutes later, a notification bubble appeared in the upper right corner of the screen. I clicked on it, and another program opened up, with a white box taking up a third of the screen. There were several lines of what appeared to be gibberish. Numbers and letters that I assumed correlated in some encrypted digital filing system. All but one were grayed out. I clicked the one that wasn't.

"Son of a bitch."

The target's face was all too familiar to me.

Clarissa.

I stood and walked over to the mirror next to the front door. For the next few minutes, I stared at myself, noting the new lines etched into the corners of my eyes. The gray whiskers on my face. The scratches that were taking longer than usual to heal. Then I cleared my mind and thought about what to do next. There was one option.

I had to let this play out. The person on the other end of that communication had been the one to place the hit on me. I was close. So close I could picture wrapping my hands around the guy's throat and choking the life out of him. It was time to put an end to this.

Then and there, I assumed a new legend.

I was to become Dylan Van de Berg.

I would have my vengeance.

Jack's story continues in **NOBLE REVENGE**. *Pre-order now:*
https://www.amazon.com/dp/B09YPBWZ9Z

Join the LT Ryan reader family & receive a free copy of the Jack Noble story, *The Recruit*. Click the link below to get started:
https://ltryan.com/jack-noble-newsletter-signup-1

ALSO BY L.T. RYAN

Visit https://ltryan.com/pb for paperback purchasing information.

The Jack Noble Series

The Recruit (Short Story)

The First Deception (Prequel 1)

Noble Beginnings (Jack Noble #1)

A Deadly Distance (Jack Noble #2)

Thin Line (Jack Noble #3)

Noble Intentions (Jack Noble #4)

When Dead in Greece (Jack Noble #5)

Noble Retribution (Jack Noble #6)

Noble Betrayal (Jack Noble #7)

Never Go Home (Jack Noble #8)

Beyond Betrayal (Clarissa Abbot)

Noble Judgment (Jack Noble #9)

Never Cry Mercy (Jack Noble #10)

Deadline (Jack Noble #11)

End Game (Jack Noble #12)

Noble Ultimatum (Jack Noble #13)

Noble Legend (Jack Noble #14)

Noble Revenge (Jack Noble #15) - coming soon

Bear Logan Series

Ripple Effect

Blowback

Take Down

Deep State

Rachel Hatch Series

Drift

Downburst

Fever Burn

Smoke Signal

Firewalk - December 2020

Whitewater - March 2021

Mitch Tanner Series

The Depth of Darkness

Into The Darkness

Deliver Us From Darkness - coming Summer 2021

Cassie Quinn Series

Path of Bones

Untitled - February, 2021

Blake Brier Series

Unmasked

Unleashed - January, 2021

Untitled - April, 2021

Affliction Z Series

Affliction Z: Patient Zero

Affliction Z: Abandoned Hope

ABOUT THE AUTHOR

L.T. Ryan is a *USA Today* and international bestselling author. The new age of publishing offered L.T. the opportunity to blend his passions for creating, marketing, and technology to reach audiences with his popular Jack Noble series.

Living in central Virginia with his wife, the youngest of his three daughters, and their three dogs, L.T. enjoys staring out his window at the trees and mountains while he should be writing, as well as reading, hiking, running, and playing with gadgets. See what he's up to at http://ltryan.com.

Social Medial Links:

- Facebook (L.T. Ryan): https://www.facebook.com/LTRyanAuthor

- Facebook (Jack Noble Page): https://www.facebook.com/JackNobleBooks/

- Twitter: https://twitter.com/LTRyanWrites

- Goodreads: http://www.goodreads.com/author/show/6151659.L_T_Ryan

Printed in Great Britain
by Amazon